BEHIND HIS EYES

THE JETTY BEACH SERIES BOOK 1

CLAIRE KINGSLEY

Always Have LLC

Copyright © 2016 Claire Kingsley

All rights reserved.

No part of this book may be reproduced in any form or by any electronic or mechanical means, including information storage and retrieval systems, without written permission from the author, except for the use of brief quotations in a book review.

This is a work of fiction. Any names, characters, places, or incidents are products of the author's imagination and used in a fictitious manner. Any resemblance to actual people, places, or events is purely coincidental or fictionalized.

Edited by Larks and Katydids

Cover by Kari March Designs

Published by Always Have, LLC

Previously published as Must Be Love: A Jetty Beach Romance

ISBN: 9781797049250

www.clairekingsleybooks.com

❦ Created with Vellum

ABOUT THIS BOOK

Behind His Eyes was previously published as Must Be Love: A Jetty Beach Romance.

Some wounds only love can heal

I never thought Nicole Prescott would walk back into my life—adorably drunk and dropping things, no less. But here she is, more beautiful than I remember.

She's been hurt, and I understand pain all too well. But I shouldn't be the guy to help her through it. I came home to get my own life together. I can't pick up the pieces of hers.

Ryan Jacobsen and I were kids together, but he's all man, now. Sexy and sweet, with brooding green eyes that hide a universe of secrets.

His stubbly jaw, delicious abs, and artistic soul make him irresistible. (And have I mentioned the things he can do with his tongue?) My heart—and my body—want more. They want everything.

Although the gravity between us is inescapable, he tries to push me away. The pain behind his eyes holds him back, and it just might tear us apart.

1

NICOLE

By the time I realize I'm drunk, it's too late.

"I really love you. Do you know that?" I lean my head against Melissa's shoulder.

Melissa has been my best friend since forever. My mom still keeps a faded picture on the fridge—the two of us as toddlers, dressed in matching splatter-paint t-shirts and neon pink bike shorts, ridiculous spiky pigtails sticking out at all angles.

"I know, baby." She pats me on the hand like a mother coaxing a child into bed.

Our waitress sidles up to the table with a cheery smile plastered to her face. "Can I get you ladies anything else?"

"You are just the cutest. Didn't I used to babysit you when you were like, this high?" I hold out my hand, finding it surprisingly hard to keep it steady. "You're so pretty."

"Okay, I think we're ready for the check." Melissa scoots what's left of my mojito across the table.

"Hey!"

The waitress nods and scampers off.

"You took my drink." I slump down into the booth,

despondent. "Why are we here, anyway? I hate this restaurant."

I worked in this restaurant for two summers during high school. The Porthole Inn. What does that mean, anyway? Like half the places in Jetty Beach, it's strewn with nautical decorations. Rope and old ship's wheels hang from the wood paneled walls, and half the light fixtures are old lanterns. A faded life preserver greets customers when they walk in the door.

"If you hate this restaurant, why did you suggest it?" Melissa asks, fiddling with the zipper on her hoodie. She's dressed in a pair of distressed jeans and a black tank top, her hoodie falling carelessly from her slim shoulders. She's probably even wearing flip flops, but of course she looks amazing. Melissa makes anything look good.

"Why are you so gorgeous?"

"You're drunk."

"I am not."

"You so are. You always start telling everyone how gorgeous they are when you're drunk."

"I do not." Of course, she's right; I totally do. "Why aren't you drunk? I shouldn't be doing this alone."

"You probably shouldn't be doing this at all. What am I going to tell your parents?"

I blow out a breath through pursed lips, spraying spit onto the table. For reasons only rum can tell, I find that hilarious, and cover my mouth to stifle a fit of giggles.

"At least you're in a better mood," she says.

"I'm always in a good mood."

Okay, so that's not quite true. I've been in a terrible mood. But who can blame me? I'm back in the tiny beach town where I grew up. Worse than that, at twenty-seven, I'm crashing at my parents' house. Despite rumors to the contrary, my generation are not a bunch of freeloaders who are happy to live off mommy and daddy forever. I'm an independent woman. I made a life for myself, away from this town. I was going places. Until—

A sob bursts from my mouth, my mojito-induced good mood skittering away in the face of my awful reality.

"Honey," Melissa says, patting my back.

It occurs to me that I can't remember when she moved from her seat across the table to sit next to me.

"What am I going to do, Melissa?" I ask between breaths. "This is the worst thing that's ever happened to me."

"Actually, it's probably the best thing that's ever happened to you. You just don't realize it yet."

"That isn't possible," I say, although it comes out sounding more like *pobbible*. I lean forward and put my head down on the table.

I can't seem to get over the feeling that my world has utterly collapsed. A week ago, I was sitting at work, doing my job, wondering what my boyfriend Jason and I were going to do on Friday night. Hours later, I got home to find another woman straddling him. Naked. Very naked.

The sense of hopelessness is so pervasive, there are days I can barely be bothered to get off the couch. Melissa came over earlier and literally dragged me to the bathroom to shower, claiming what I needed was to get out of the house. Considering it's my parents' house, she was probably right. But now that I'm sitting in a booth in the stupid Porthole Inn, a place Jason and I went to before almost every stupid high school dance, I don't think it was such a great plan.

My stomach churns and suddenly the five mojitos don't seem like such a great plan either. Was it five? Or were there six? I honestly have no idea.

"Jason is a douche," Melissa says. "That jackass can rot in hell."

I sit up and swipe a hand under my nose. "He is a dickwad."

"Damn right he is. Atta girl."

I sniff again and take a sip of water. I thought Jason was the love of my life. Everything was perfect. He was the hot football player every girl wanted—and he picked me. We dated for two years, and then he got a football scholarship to Linfield. Sure, it was a small college, and it meant moving to Oregon, but Jason and I were meant to be together. He seemed excited when I decided to go with him to Linfield. We had a lot of fun in those days. We partied some, and did the whole college thing.

After graduation, I was expecting a proposal. After all, isn't that how it works? High school, college, careers, marriage? He got a job with a big insurance company in Seattle, and I was happy to move back to Washington. I started with an event planning and PR company, we got an apartment in the city, and life was good. Sure, he was moody sometimes, and maybe we fought a little. But he missed football, so I understood. Going from college to adult life was a big deal. He just needed time.

Five years later, and still no ring? I should have at least started to wonder.

Melissa raises her glass—is that still her first drink?— and hands me my water. "No more dipshits!"

I lift my glass. "No more dipshits!"

The waitress returns and slips the bill onto the table. Melissa plunks a credit card onto the black plastic tray. "I got this."

"No." I fumble with my purse. "I can pay."

"Nicole Marie Prescott," she says, using her teacher voice.

"Yes, Ms. Simon?"

She smacks me across the arm.

"Ouch!" I rub the skin as if she's hurt me and stick out my lower lip, but the sting actually feels good. Better than the empty feeling in my chest.

"The least I can do is buy you a few drinks. Or maybe it was more than a few" She spins the bill around to look at it more closely.

"I'm sorry."

"It's fine, Nic. I just ... I don't know what else to do for you. We've binged on ice cream, burned his sweatshirt on the beach, drank our fucking weight in wine, and if I have to watch *The Notebook* even one more time, I am literally going to stab out my own eyeballs."

Tears flood my eyes and run down my face. "They died together, Mel." Sniff, sob. "He loved her so much they died together."

My shoulders shake with sobs and Melissa rubs slow circles across my back.

"Holy shit, Nicole, pull yourself together." She lifts my chin and wipes beneath my eyes, then holds up her finger. It's smudged with black mascara. "You look like hell."

I sniff again. "I don't care."

"Yeah, well, you probably should. Come on, let's go to the bathroom and get you cleaned up before someone sees you like this. If you need to ugly-cry, we'll do it in private, m'kay?"

Coming from anyone else, that would probably hurt, but even drunk as I am, I know what she means. I'd do the same for her.

She shuffles me to the bathroom, holding tight to my arm so I won't stumble. It's a Tuesday night, and early spring, so the Porthole is practically empty. During the tourist season, it would be packed even on a weeknight, but we more or less have the place to ourselves. Something in the back of my mind tells me I'll be grateful for that fact in the morning.

I'm not as unstable as I thought I might be. The floor stops trying to trip me after my first few steps, and although my head is fuzzy, I can walk kind of straight. Melissa ushers me through the door to the ladies' room, letting it bang shut behind her.

The face that stares at me from the smudged mirror is not a pretty one. Mascara runs in little black rivulets down my face, and I left most of my lipstick on my mojito glasses. Melissa takes a wet tissue and tries to mop up the damage. I stand there, pouting while she wipes beneath my eyes.

All at once, my bladder clenches. My knees buckle and I grab my crotch. "I have to pee."

"Go." Melissa pushes me toward the stall.

I can't figure out the latch, and my bladder feels like it's going to explode. This is how I'm going to go. Not wrapped in the arms of my soulmate, passing peacefully into the next life with my one true love. Nope. I'm going to die on the bathroom floor at the Porthole Inn because I can't close the stall door and my bladder explodes.

"Oh for fuck's sake, I'll hold the door," Melissa says.

I fumble with my jeans, pull them down, and sit. Bliss. I gasp, unsure for a second as to whether I've managed to get my panties down.

"You okay in there?"

"Yeah." Panties, check. "Just ... never mind."

Melissa's phone goes off, blaring out some ridiculous dubstep music. "Nic, you okay? I gotta take this. I'll be outside."

The stall door shifts a little and I hear her flip-flops flapping as she leaves. I finish, pull up my jeans, and pay extra attention to make sure they're properly buttoned and zipped —I'm not that drunk. After washing my hands, I shoulder my little black purse and wander out in search of Melissa.

I shuffle outside, making an effort to appear as not-drunk as possible, a ruse which any sober person can probably see through in an instant. The waitress glances up at me as I push open the front door, her teenage eyes full of judgment.

Just wait, sweetie. Life seems all perfect now, with your perky boobs and teeth that haven't started to go crooked because of years without your retainer. One day you'll be stumbling out of the Porthole Inn, drunk as shit because the love of your life trampled on your heart, and everyone in this town will know all about it. I am your future.

I trip through the door, over absolutely nothing except my own feet. Melissa is nowhere to be seen. I know she wouldn't leave me here without a ride. Granted, I can practically walk home; it isn't like Jetty Beach is very big. You can walk a lot of places, and my parents' house is close to the area affectionately known as downtown.

Having spent the last several years living in Seattle, I can't help but see Jetty Beach as nothing more than a village. Downtown? There isn't even a stoplight. The only tall buildings are the beachside hotels and a few big timeshares north of town. Downtown is full of little stores selling beachy decor and kites, and a few restaurants. Nothing much.

But despite the proximity to my folks, I realize pretty quickly that walking home isn't an option—even if Melissa has suddenly turned into a different person and left me here. Half the town would see me stumble home, and by morning I'd be the subject of all the gossip.

Did you see Nicole Prescott last night? She was walking

home, but she'd clearly been drinking. Poor girl. You heard what happened with Jason, of course. Yep, it's true. The golden couple no more. Well, they say there was another woman, but Nicole obviously did something to make him stray. Who can blame him, really?

Motherfucking Jason. Everyone loves him. He was Jetty Beach's golden boy. His father is the only lawyer in a thirty-mile radius, so he might as well be royalty. Jason was the star of the town, the hometown hero. Football player, perfect grades, perfect smile, and that perfect ass.

He and I made sense, really. I was his counterpart. I wasn't a star athlete, but I played varsity volleyball. My grades were stellar. I had my shit together. I knew where I was going with my life, I had a plan, and I was going to see it through. People expected me to do well, to do the right thing, to excel.

And everything was going along perfectly until Jason messed it all up.

I realize tears are burning my eyes again. Where the hell is Melissa? Sniffing hard and running my sleeve over my nose, I walk across the parking lot to her car. I just want to get home, bury my drunk head in a pillow, and sleep.

Of course, Melissa is nowhere in sight. I fumble with my purse to get out my phone, leaning against her car for balance. The zipper sticks and my lack of ability to extricate my phone from my purse sends a whirlwind of anger running through me. It's Jason's fault. I'm standing alone in the parking lot of the stupid Porthole Inn, in stupid Jetty Beach, my phone held captive by my purse, because Jason was cheating on me.

Tears stream down my face—tears of anger this time, rather than pathetic dejection. Gritting my teeth, I kick a rock, only realizing *after* I smash my toe that I'm wearing open sandals.

"Oh my fucking ouch!"

I lift my foot, awkwardly hopping on the other one, and try to grab my throbbing toe. Not a good idea when you've had four mojitos. Or was it five? Six?

Just as I'm about to tip over and hit the pavement, a strong hand grips my elbow. My purse falls, the zipper magically opening in midair, and spills its contents all over the parking lot.

It takes me much longer than it should to realize what's happening. I watch my wallet, lipstick, old receipts, and who knows what else clatter across the ground while someone gently grabs both my arms and keeps me from falling.

"Oh no." I mumble something and try to straighten. I tip again, staggering a little, but the hands hold me steady.

"I've got you."

I don't recognize the voice, but it's deep and melodic—just the slightest bit raspy. I look up and blink hard, and the face looking down at me makes me feel like I've swallowed my own tongue.

Ryan Jacobsen?

2

NICOLE

My breath catches in my throat and my stomach flutters. I haven't seen Ryan in years. He stands there, all grown up, looking like a man, and something about that doesn't make any sense. Light stubble covers his jaw and tousled dark hair falls down over his forehead just a bit. His white t-shirt stretches over a strong chest and broad shoulders. His green eyes squint just a little as he smiles a crooked grin at me.

I've known Ryan almost as long as Melissa, but in my memory of him, he's still the kid who didn't quite go through puberty the way the rest of the boys did. Vaguely, I recall my mom discussing him with someone else's mother, calling him a *late bloomer*.

Apparently, sometime in the last ten years, he bloomed.

I realize far too late that I'm staring at him with an open mouth.

"Hey," he says, and his voice sends a shiver up my back. *Come on, Nicole. This is Ryan Jacobsen, not some hot guy you just met.*

But damn, he is hot.

Or maybe I'm that drunk.

"Hey." It occurs to me that I must look like a mess. I swipe my fingers under my eyes and tuck my hair behind my ear, as if any of that would help.

"Are you okay?"

There's concern in his voice and it almost undoes me, sends me back to crying. But suddenly I desperately do not want to be a drunk sobbing mess in front of Ryan.

"Yeah, I'm fine," I say, trying as hard as I can to speak without slurring. "Just ... looking for Melissa."

"Right." His eyes linger on my face, his expression mystified.

His hands are still on my arms, although I'm standing without his help. As if he just notices he's still touching me, he quickly withdraws, leaving hot spots on my skin. My stomach flutters again, and I know my face is flushing red. Damn alabaster skin.

"You dropped your purse." He goes down on one knee and scoops the contents of my handbag back through the opening, then looks up at me.

There's something about him, down on his knee, grinning at me with that crazy hot smile...

Wait, Nicole. It's Ryan. Ryan Jacobsen. We played on the school playground together.

Then why am I suddenly feeling all hot between the legs?

I flush redder, my face utterly burning. "Thanks. You're beautiful. I mean ... wait, what?"

His grin broadens. He hands me my purse and stands, running a hand through his dark hair.

"Um, thanks." I take the purse from him.

"I heard you were back in town."

"Yeah. Just for now, I guess. What are you doing here?"

That smile again. "I live here."

"You ... oh." I thought Ryan moved away. He did, right after high school. I'm sure of it. "Did you move back?"

He nods. "About six months ago."

My eyes drift to the tattoos on his arms. One peeks out beneath his t-shirt and he has another on his other forearm. He has this look about him, now. I can't reconcile the fact that this is the same Ryan I grew up with. And it isn't just because I'm drunk. In fact, I'm sobering up pretty quickly.

"Why?"

His mouth drops open just a little, a flash of surprise moving across his face.

Crap, I insulted him.

"No, that's not what I mean. I meant when. Except you already said six months ago." This is not going well. But this isn't something that needs to go well, so what am I so worried about? Shouldering my purse, I look around. "Have you seen Melissa Simon? I was here with her, and she got a phone call."

"I haven't seen her. Do you need a ride home?"

As if on cue, my phone dings. I dig into my purse and fish it out, managing to keep from dropping it.

The text is from Melissa. *Where are you?*

"Um." I tap out a quick reply. *Parking lot.* "I don't think so. She just texted."

Ryan's eyes rove over me. I can't read his expression, but suddenly I very much wished Melissa *had* ditched me and I *did* need a ride home.

"I'll wait with you until she comes out, then."

"Thanks."

I need water. And a bed. I can already tell I'm going to feel like hell in the morning, and I hate the way my head is swimming. I feel like I'm missing something, like I should say something clever. Or funny. Why is Ryan Jacobsen standing in front of me in the parking lot of the Porthole Inn? And why do my eyes keep wanting to drift down to the bulge in his jeans?

Forcing my eyes back to Ryan's face doesn't help. He really is gorgeous. He has this look of either bewilderment or scathing judgment; I can't quite tell which. Maybe the scathing judgment is only in my head, but immediately I start imagining what he must be thinking of me. *Poor Nicole Prescott. Dumped and sent crawling back to Jetty Beach.*

Oh lord, it's pity. He feels sorry for me.

"There you are!" Melissa bursts out of the restaurant and runs across the parking lot. "I was looking all over for you."

"Where did you think I'd go?"

"I don't know, mojito girl. Hey, Ryan."

Ryan gives her a crooked smile, his dimples puckering. "Are you going to take her home?"

"Obviously. Drunky McDrunkerson here needs to go to bed."

"What the hell, Melissa?"

"Okay, if you're sure you've got her," Ryan says.

"Yeah, I've got her. Thanks."

Ryan grins again. "Well then, ladies. You two have a good evening. Good to see you again, Nicole."

"You too."

I watch him walk away. His jeans cup his ass perfectly. Not too tight, like some wannabe hipster, but tight enough to show off the goods.

"Hello." Melissa waves a hand in front of my face. "Earth to Nicole. Quit staring at Ryan's ass."

"I wasn't."

"Uh, yeah you were. I mean, he does have a nice ass." She tilts her head, getting her own look at it. "But come on, it's Ryan."

Yeah. It's Ryan.

Melissa ushers me into her car then gets in.

"So he's back in town?"

"Yep." She casts a weird look my direction. "Maybe six months ago? He bought that old church just north of town, the one on the bluff."

"He lives there?"

"I guess. I hear he's been fixing it up."

"I thought he moved to L.A."

"He did, but he came back."

I groan. "Ugh, why?"

Melissa casts another sidelong glance at me. "Not everyone hates this town as much as you do."

I let out a sigh. "I'm sorry, Mel. I didn't mean it like that. I don't hate this town."

Melissa came right back to Jetty Beach after getting her teaching degree, and now she wrangles fifth graders at the same elementary school we went to. I don't quite understand why, but Melissa loves Jetty Beach. It makes her happy.

"It's okay. Besides, I know where we can direct all of our seething ire."

"Jason the Jackass?"

"That's good, I like that." She puts the car in gear and backs out of her spot. "I think at this point we can both admit, getting out of the house wasn't what you needed tonight."

I shrug, fumbling with the seat belt.

Maybe not. But then again, maybe it was just the thing.

3

RYAN

Nicole Prescott.

When I decided to run into town for a few things, she was the last person I expected to see.

I saw her stumble out of the Porthole Inn, clearly more drunk than not. She looked great, of course. She always did. Her shirt was sort of careless, a bit of it tucked into her jeans, the rest hanging loose, hinting at her curves. Her hair was a mess, but all I could think about was how that's what she would look like after a night of fucking her.

Great, two seconds into seeing my childhood friend, and was already imagining her naked in my bed. I should *not* be thinking of Nicole that way.

I shouldn't be thinking of any woman that way.

I haven't seen her in about three years. The last time, she literally didn't see me. We were in a coffee shop in Seattle and she looked right through me—no recognition whatsoever. I was all set to smile and say hi, see if she wanted to catch up. She was alone, no sign of douchebag Jason. But her eyes passed over me and she walked right by, as if I wasn't even there. I was too surprised to say anything. I wasn't expecting her to jump in my arms or anything, but shit, we'd known each other since we were kids.

Of course, I do look different. Apparently more so than I realized.

I walk away from the restaurant, wishing Melissa hadn't shown up. No, it was good Melissa showed up. Nicole was drunk. The way she looked at me told me I needed to get the hell out of there, immediately. The last thing I need is to get involved with a local girl. Or any girl.

I don't pay much attention to town gossip, but I heard Nicole was back in town. I'll have to ask my mother why—she'll certainly know. I wonder if it has anything to do with douchebag Jason. Maybe she left him.

I don't hold out much hope. When Nicole and Jason didn't break up in college, I figured that was it. They'd get married and have little blond-haired douchebag kids. She seemed happy, I guess. I wouldn't really know. We hung out as kids, but somewhere around puberty, we drifted apart. I was the awkward skinny kid who didn't grow facial hair until I was almost nineteen. She developed early and had every boy in town jacking off to fantasies of her.

It wasn't much of a surprise when she and Jason started dating—and I couldn't pinpoint why, but it never sat well with me. By then, our friendship was nothing but a memory, something that happened to people who were so different, we didn't even know each other anymore. I wasn't jealous, exactly. But Jason was a cocky asshole, and I knew he'd never be good enough for her. Unfortunately, it wasn't my call.

Now she's back. By the state of her makeup, she was crying. I shouldn't care why. Nicole isn't mine to worry over.

I have enough to deal with in my own life. I'm doing really well, and I don't want to shake things up.

Still, just the sight of her got me hard. What was that about? I adjust my pants as I walk away. I told myself already, I need to back off, and do it now. Despite the way she made me stand at attention, I know I can't get involved with someone right now. Or maybe ever. I moved home to Jetty Beach to get better. The slower pace of life is good for me, as is living near my family. I've made a lot of progress, but I'm not ready to let someone in again. I doubt I ever will be.

Even if that woman is Nicole Prescott. And she looked like a beautiful drunk angel.

I hop in my car and head north, out of town. The drive to my house isn't long. It isn't a house in the traditional sense, but I'm not a traditional guy. I bought an old abandoned church when I moved back to the beach, and spent the last six months renovating. My parents think I'm nuts, but they never really understood me.

My dad refers to me as the "artsy-fartsy one." My mom is just happy to have me living close enough to check on me constantly. As far as the building, the bones are good, and the lighting—oh my god, the lighting. Huge windows look out on the ocean on the back side, these gorgeous things with peaked tops and original glass. As a photographer, I'm a bit obsessed with lighting. The way the sun streams through those windows is perfect. I tried explaining that to my dad when I bought the place, and he nodded appreciatively. He didn't really understand, but I didn't expect him to. He still thinks I'm just messing around with my camera, and probably wonders when I'm going to get a real job.

My phone rings and I answer through the Bluetooth. "Hey, Mom."

"Sweetie, where are you? Are you home?"

I thought moving back to Jetty Beach might mean my mom didn't check up on me so often, but that isn't the case. She calls me at least once a day. I know she has her reasons. It doesn't seem to matter how often I assure her I'm okay. I'm pretty sure she believes me when I say I'm fine, but she seems afraid it won't last. Hell, I'm afraid of the same thing sometimes.

"I'm good. I'm heading home now. I'll be there soon."

"That's good to hear."

"Do you need something, or are you just calling to check up on me?" I tried to show my mom how to text so she could send me a quick message if she just needed reassurance. Technology is not her thing. I'm pretty sure she was born in the wrong era. She belongs in the fifties or something.

"I made pie."

"That's great, Mom." She's always baking something. "It's kind of late for me to come over, don't you think?"

"Yes, it's late. I'm headed to bed soon."

So why did you call me to tell me you made pie?

"All right." Before I can stop myself, I ask about Nicole. "Hey, Mom, I ran into Nicole Prescott tonight. Did you hear she's back in town?"

"I sure did," she says. I recognize the sound of her conspiratorial voice. Yep, she knows exactly what's going on. "I saw her mother the other day at the bank. Apparently Nicole and that Jason boy she was dating broke up."

"He's not really a boy anymore," I say, although try convincing my mom of that. Everyone under thirty is still a kid as far as she is concerned. I hesitate. I don't need to know. But I have to ask. "Did you hear why?"

"I think there was another girl."

Anger rolls through my chest. He cheated on Nicole? Who does that?

Douchebag Jason, apparently.

"That sucks."

"Did you remember about the meeting?" Mom asks.

"Meeting?"

She lets out an exasperated sigh. "Yes, Ryan. Meeting. You agreed to help run the Jetty Beach Art Festival, remember?"

I groan. I did agree to that, didn't I? I was having a few beers with my dad when Mom brought it up, so it didn't seem like such a bad idea at the time. Jetty Beach has an art festival every year. It used to be run by the owner of the largest art gallery in town, but he retired last year. The committee still wants the event to continue, but they need more volunteers. I'm pretty sure my mom volunteered me before she even told me about it. She was rather adamant that I agree.

"Mom, I'm not sure I have time for this right now."

"Oh, nonsense."

"There's a lot of work to do on the church building. There's literally a hole in the wall near my bed. I can see outside."

"You have plenty of time," she says with a little laugh. "I think this will be good for you. Besides, this is an art festival. Isn't this your area? Maybe you could show some of your photographs."

I grin despite myself. I have some photographs I can certainly display, but most of my work is not something I'd show my mother. "I don't know."

"The meeting is tomorrow, honey. It's at the Old Town Café. Ten o'clock."

I pull up the long driveway, my tires crunching on the gravel. "Okay, okay, Mom."

"Good. Love you, baby boy."

"Love you too, Mom."

I grab my jacket and go inside, tossing my wallet and phone onto a side table near the door. The air is cold, but man I love this place. The high ceiling with exposed wood beams, the tall windows, the gorgeous hardwood floors. There are a hundred perfect places to shoot. Word got around to some of my past clients that I have this great studio, and I'm having no problem getting people to drive out here for photo shoots.

The ocean waves are muffled, but I can hear their steady rhythm through the walls. My mind drifts back to Nicole, tear-streaked and despondent. I know what it feels like to have your heart crushed. Jason might be a douchebag, but she was with him a long time. She must be pretty devastated.

Yet there was something in her eyes—a fire in her. I felt it in her gaze when she looked at me. And the way her skin felt when I grabbed her so she wouldn't fall.

I run a hand through my hair and adjust my pants again. Damn it, why is every thought of Nicole getting me hard?

I walk through the studio to the doorway that leads to my apartment, off the side of the main building. It's small—a sitting area, a compact kitchen, and a bathroom through another door. My king-size bed looks a little ridiculous in the middle of the room, but I like having a lot of space to stretch out, so I made it fit. Besides, it's just me. I don't need much room.

I wonder if Nicole made it home okay. I take off my shirt, toss it in a basket, and pull a pair of sweats from my dresser. I glance at the letter I left sitting there, unopened. I've had it for a long time. Maybe soon I'll be able to bring myself to open it.

Not today.

I shake my head and drop my jeans, then pull on my sweats. I have to put Nicole out of my mind, and keep her there. I need to stay focused on myself. On staying healthy. I feel bad for her, but she'll be fine—and if she isn't, I'm the last thing she needs.

4

NICOLE

Morning comes far too early. My phone, dinging with emails, wakes me well before I'm ready to crack my eyes open. My head hurts, and my mouth tastes nasty, but considering I dropped into bed still in my clothes, it could be worse. I grab my phone from the nightstand. Twelve emails already, half of them from my boss, Sandra.

"Okay, okay, I'm up."

Sandra has been great about the whole mess. I actually broke down crying in her office after I found out about Jason. I probably should have called in sick that day. Coming home to another woman straddling your boyfriend in your bed should qualify you for sick leave, right? I tried to soldier on, hoping work would keep my mind off the fact that my life had exploded.

Later that afternoon, I found myself sobbing on the other side of Sandra's desk. She offered to let me go home, but I didn't have a home to go to. My home was Jason's home, and that wasn't going to work. In the end, I arranged to work remotely for a couple of weeks while I figured things out. I packed a bunch of clothes and drove to my parents' house.

It's been a few days, and I definitely need to start getting my life back together. The weeknight drinking isn't helping.

I tap out a few quick replies, and haul myself out of bed. My hair is a disaster, matted with last night's hairspray, but I don't bother with it yet. I just need to get some work done. I grab my laptop and leave it on the kitchen island while I go in search of something caffeinated.

Without much hope, I dig through the cupboards. After my mom turned fifty, she became some kind of health nut. My dad grumbles about it, but even he has to admit the two of them look better than they have in years. My mom runs a lot, and does yoga. I don't mind not having pasta or bread in the house, but the shocking lack of coffee is getting ridiculous. She even tossed her coffee maker. I'm going to have to go buy a French press or something, because this no coffee thing is not okay.

"Morning." My mom's concerned voice comes from behind me as I rifle through another cupboard.

"Morning." I give up on my quest for caffeine and sit down at the island with my laptop. "How do I have seven new emails? I just checked five minutes ago."

"Can I get you something?"

"Coffee?"

She presses her lips into a little smile. Her hair is pulled up in a bun, and I can see the streaks of gray in her dark blond hair. She's dressed in a tank top and yoga pants, her feet bare.

"Aren't you going to work?" I ask.

"Not today. I'm taking your dad to the doctor later, so I took the whole day off."

"The doctor? Why? Is Dad okay?"

My dad is a contractor. He built half the houses in Jetty Beach. Dad grew up in Orlando, and Mom calls him her city boy, but he loves small town life. He's a hard-working man, his hands rough and calloused from years of swinging a hammer. Aside from the time our whole family got the flu when I was ten, I can't remember my dad ever being sick.

"Oh, he's fine. He's had some shoulder pain lately so I finally convinced him to get it looked at. But we both know he'll skip the appointment if I don't go with him."

I smile. That is certainly true. "Okay, but seriously, Mom. This moratorium on coffee has got to stop, at least while I'm here."

Mom pulls out a barstool and sits, resting her elbows on the kitchen island. Dad remodeled the kitchen a few years ago, with beautiful white marble countertops and custom cabinets.

"How long do you think that will be, honey?"

I freeze. I've only been home for a few days. Has it been more? I glance over at the calendar hanging on the wall. What day is it?

"I don't know," I say, feeling defensive. "My life sort of got dumped in the toilet. Are you anxious to get rid of me?"

"No, of course we don't want to get rid of you. We just want to make sure you have a plan."

I gaze at my laptop screen. She's right. I need a plan. I love plans. Checklists, spreadsheets, timelines. I am literally passionate about that stuff. But for the first time in my life, I don't have any of it.

"I..." I trail off, unsure of what to say. "Look, I just need a little time to figure things out. And I have a lot of work to do."

"I know you do." She tilts her head and gives me her

mom smile, the one that hasn't changed since I was little. "Did you have a nice time with Melissa last night?"

And there she is. Judging me. I'm sure of it. "Yeah, it was fine."

"You feel okay?"

"I drank too much and now I have to answer emails from people who should know how to do their jobs but are inexplicably incompetent."

The silence stretches out and Mom just sits there. That means she has something to tell me.

"So..." she says.

I finish typing out a reply. "Yes?"

She doesn't answer.

"Mom, what?"

"I have a suggestion."

I already don't like where this is going. "I'm listening."

"I was talking with Howard Nelson. He used to own the Sunset Gallery, over on Main Street."

"Used to own?"

"He retired last year," Mom says. "I told you about that."

I shrug. She probably did, but I don't pay close attention when she tells me the local news of the day.

"In any case, Howard isn't able to run the art festival anymore. He's nearly eighty. They have a small committee, but no one has any real experience running an event. I thought, with your experience..."

"My experience?" I do work on a lot of events, but I'm certainly not responsible for running any of them. Not even close. Despite my recent promotion to Events Manager, my job is actually quite tedious. On paper, it looks great. Our firm works with a lot of big companies and non-profits. I get to rub elbows with wealthy businesspeople, and whenever I tell people what I do, it sounds impressive. But the actual day-to-day work isn't very interesting.

"Sure, you're perfect for this. What do you think?"

I blink at her, my non-caffeinated brain having a tough time catching up. "Think about what?"

"About volunteering to run the art festival?"

"Run it? Mom, I don't even know how long I'll be in town. And despite the current state of my hair, I'm still working. I have a lot to do."

"I know, honey, but I thought this might give you something else to focus on. How much can you really get done just from your laptop anyway?"

She's right, to a point. "When is this thing, anyway?"

"The meeting is at ten."

I sigh. "I'm sure the existing committee is fine. They know how to do things. I'd only be in the way."

Mom drums her nails on the countertop. "Well ... not really. Apparently they're having a hard time getting things going. In fact, that's why I told them you'd help. They're really desperate."

"You already told them?" I throw up my hands, rolling my eyes so hard I practically see the inside of my skull. "Seriously, Mom? I'm here, what, a few days, and I've already been volun-told?"

"Volun-told? That's not even a word."

"It is definitely a word."

She puts a hand on my back. "Howard Nelson will be absolutely crushed if the festival dies out. He feels so guilty for leaving it to others, but he can't keep pushing himself so hard. They need someone who knows what they're doing. Besides, this will get you out and about a little bit."

"Is that what this is about? Trying to get me out of your house?"

"It would be a start." There is humor in her voice and she gives me a little smile. "Honey, your dad and I are worried about you. I know this breakup with Jason is hard, and believe me, we're glad you came home."

I raise an eyebrow.

"I'm being serious, Nicole. There are few things harder on a mother than watching her child suffer. You'll understand that someday." She stands and touches her hand to my cheek. It's soft and cool. "You're hurting, and that's to be expected. But staring at your laptop, and lying around watching movies with Melissa isn't going to help you get better. You need to get out a little bit. Maybe even go on a few dates."

"Dates?" I pull away. "Really, Mom?"

"It doesn't have to be anything serious, honey. I bet Melissa would agree with me."

I sigh. She's right, Melissa would agree. She's already been hinting at it. But who the hell would I date in this town?

Don't think about Ryan. Don't think about Ryan.

"Your face is flushing," she says.

"It's hot in here. And I need coffee."

"That's perfect. The planning meeting is at Old Town Café. Don't they have great coffee?"

I close my eyes and pinch the bridge of my nose. My headache is getting worse. "Fine. I'll go. I'm not committing to anything, though. I'll just go talk to them and see what they need."

She pats my cheek. "Good girl. But, honey," she says, and wrinkles her nose, "make sure you shower first."

"I'm only doing this for the coffee," I say to her back as she walks away.

An art festival. I have no idea how to put together an art festival. There can't be much to it, and the rest of the volunteers will know what to do. Maybe Mom is right. Maybe I do need something to take my mind off Jason.

And off Ryan, too.

5

RYAN

A litany of excuses runs through my head on the drive into town. Why did I let my mom talk me into this? I have no interest in helping organize an art festival. I don't care if this is "my area." I wasn't kidding when I told her I have a lot of work to do on the church. There really is a hole in the wall that needs patching, and a million other projects besides. Not to mention photo shoots. I have clients to take care of.

I know what my mom is doing. She has it in her head that I need to get out more. I know she worries—that's what moms do—but I try to assure her I'm doing fine. I don't need her inventing ways to get me out of the house. I guess the good news is, she isn't trying to set me up with women. Volunteering me for local events is bad enough.

The remodel is the most obvious excuse. That should work. I can tell them I'm swamped with renovations. I'll add a touch of altruism. *It wouldn't be fair to the committee, since I don't have the time, and the workload would have to fall to others.* It's true, for the most part. I suppose I can make time. But I don't particularly want to. I know my mom means well, but her meddling has a tendency to get me into trouble.

I park and walk into the café, the smell of fresh ground coffee wafting through the door. I'm a little early, so I figure I'll get some coffee and maybe breakfast. I glance around, looking to see if the other festival committee members have arrived yet, and stop in my tracks. Looking up at me, from behind a very large mug, is Nicole Prescott.

Of course she's here. This is Jetty Beach. We practically step on each other when we walk out the door in this town.

Her eyes catch mine and her cheeks turn the slightest shade of pink. Her blond hair is nicely blown out, falling in soft waves to her shoulders, her makeup much neater than the night before. Either way, she looks beautiful. She bites her lip and gives me a small smile.

I walk over to her table. "Hey."

"Hey." She glances down at her coffee. I can tell she's embarrassed. It's adorable.

Don't do it, Ryan. You're here for the art festival thing. Don't do it.

"Mind if I sit down?"

I did it.

"Sure, of course." Her cheeks color a little more and she brushes her hair back from her face as I take the seat across from her. "Listen, last night—"

"Don't worry about it. Believe me, I've been there."

"Not exactly my finest moment. I'm sorry you had to see me like that."

With your tousled hair and sparkling blue eyes? "Really, it was no big deal. All you did was drop your purse. Could have happened to anyone."

"Yeah, and almost fell on my face. But thanks again for your help."

"No problem."

She takes a sip of her coffee. "So, how have you been?"

"Good. You know, working, renovating the old church, that sort of thing."

"Melissa said you live out there?"

"I do. It's a little unconventional, I guess. But the interior is perfect for my business."

Her eyebrows lift. "Your business? What do you do?"

"I'm a photographer."

"Are you? I'd love to see your work sometime."

"I'd love to show it to you."

Nicole chews on her bottom lip again. Man, I love it when she does that. It makes me want to nibble on it.

"Um..." She stammers a little. "Wow, so it's kind of crazy seeing you again. I almost didn't recognize you."

"I know, look at us. All grown up." I want to ask her about Jason, but don't want to sound like a dick. Or like I'm hitting on her. "Are you back in town for a visit, or are you planning to stay a while?"

Her shoulders slump and she swallows hard. "It's just temporary. You remember Jason Baker? He and I were still dating, and, well ... we're not anymore."

Before I can think about what I'm doing, I put my hand on top of hers. It sends a little jolt of electricity through me. She twitches just slightly, but doesn't pull away. "I'm sorry."

Her lips part. Our eyes meet and I feel frozen to the spot, my hand on hers, and things stir down below.

"Oh, it's okay." She slips her hand away, breaking the spell. "Bastard was cheating on me, so good riddance."

Damn, that pisses me off. It's worse hearing it from her. "Fuck that guy." I try to backtrack by winking and giving her a little smile, so I won't come across like a total asshole. But I mean it.

The corners of her mouth turn up. "Yeah, fuck that guy."

"Ryan! Nicole! You're both here already."

I look up to find Mrs. Johnson, her lined face lit up with a wide smile. She's dressed in a peach cardigan and what my brother Cody would definitely call "mom jeans." A stick-on name tag hangs precariously from the fuzz of her sweater, *Cheryl* scrawled across it in blue sharpie. Is she wearing a name tag for this, or did she come from somewhere else?

"Hi, Mrs. Johnson," I say, slightly confused. I know Cheryl Johnson is on the festival committee, so she'll be expecting to see me, but what did she mean about Nicole being here already?

"Call me Cheryl," she says with a wave of her hand. She pulls up a chair and sits. "Good to see the both of you. Thank you so much for volunteering. I have to admit, this festival has turned into a bit of a disaster."

Nicole bites her lip again. "Mrs. Johnson—"

"Cheryl."

"Right, Cheryl. I'm not sure what my mother told you, but I'm not positive I can be of much help. I'm only in town temporarily. I'm sure it will be better for someone based here to see to most of the details."

Oh, shit. Nicole is supposed to help with this thing too?

"Nonsense," Cheryl says. "There's a lot to be done, but it isn't overwhelming. I think you'll be great."

"That's very nice of you to say, but I don't think I have time—"

"It's all right, dear," Cheryl says, interrupting. "All our committee members over the years have been volunteers. It's easy enough to work into your schedule. And we simply have to find a way to make this work. For Howard. For Jetty Beach. This event kicks off the busy season."

"Where's the rest of the committee?" I ask.

"Oh, we're the committee," Cheryl says, with a smile that crinkles the lines at the corners of her eyes.

"Just us?"

"Yep."

Nicole gapes at me, her full lips open.

"What happened to the rest of the committee?" I ask. There has to be a way out of this.

"Well, you know, over time people drop off," Cheryl says. "Joyce Merton died a few years ago, of course, and she was one of the original founders. Howard would help if he could, but his health isn't what it used to be. There were others, I suppose, but they've lost interest or moved away."

"So, you're saying the three of us are supposed to organize the entire festival?" Nicole asks, her voice going weak.

"Well, mostly the two of you, to be completely honest," Cheryl says. "My daughter and grandkids are in town this week, and we have a vacation planned, and..."

Cheryl Johnson's list of reasons she can't help with the festival fades from my hearing. I stare at Nicole. Her skin has gone ashen and her forehead is tight. She looks so stressed. I want to touch her again—wrap her in my arms and feel her body melt against mine. Explore that soft mouth with my tongue. Touch those—

"Ryan?"

"I'm sorry, what was that?" I blink at Cheryl.

"So, you're all set then? To help Nicole run the festival?" Cheryl says.

I hesitate, my gaze darting to Nicole. Her big, blue eyes plead with me. I don't want to be involved, and as tempting as she is, I don't think spending a lot of time with Nicole is a good idea. I'm still trying to pick up the pieces of my own life, and she just got out of a long-term relationship. It's a recipe for absolute disaster.

Nicole mouths *Please*, and bites that lower lip again.

Yep. I'm screwed.

"Sure," I hear my voice say. It's a little bit like an out-of-body experience. "I'll help."

Nicole visibly relaxes, and reaches across the table to touch my hand. There's that jolt of electricity again. Judging by the look in her eyes, she feels it too.

"Thank you," she says.

"This will be great!" Cheryl stands, her chair scraping across the floor. "Thank you both so much. I'll bring in my little box of festival goodies, and the two of you can get started."

I let out a breath and sit back in my chair. What did I just get myself into? More to the point, what did my mother get me into? I need to have a little chat with her later.

Nevertheless, I can't help grinning at Nicole. "I guess this calls for more coffee."

6

NICOLE

The Sunset Art Gallery has seen better days. I pull my car into the empty parking lot and gaze at the whitewashed building. It does have a beachy sort of charm, but the peeling paint on the siding and the faded trim speak of neglect. Howard Nelson opened the gallery during a time when Jetty Beach was nothing more than a tiny town with a handful of residents. Local lore claims that the first visitors to Jetty Beach came because of Howard's art gallery, and it ushered in a new era for the fledgling community.

Despite the way locals tended to gripe about tourists, particularly their inability to drive, tourism is Jetty Beach's primary industry. Without the seasonal influx of visitors, the town would quickly fade away.

The sky is a dingy gray, threatening rain, and the wind whips at the tattered windsocks hanging on the eaves outside the gallery door. I'm early, so I check my phone while I wait in the car. No new emails. That is an absolute miracle. I spent half the previous day on the phone and the other half answering a never-ending stream of emails and texts from people in the office. That didn't leave me any time to look at the box of paperwork Cheryl handed off to me. I still haven't wrapped my head around what needs to be done to get the art festival off the ground. Hopefully Ryan has more ideas than I do.

Ryan. Just the thought of him makes my heart beat a little faster. Which is, of course, ridiculous. I came back to the beach to get myself together, not hook up with some guy. I roll my eyes. As if Ryan is just some guy. When he sat with me and listened to Cheryl Johnson drop the bombshell about the disarray of the upcoming festival, I could tell he wanted to bolt. He looked like a deer trying to escape a predator.

But he stayed. The relief I felt when he agreed to help was massive. I can't believe they dropped this huge event in my lap. It isn't like I'm sitting around doing nothing. I have a job, and a life. Well, I have a job at least. The life part is debatable.

Bing. I really need to change my ringtone. I'm starting to hate that *bing* sound. It usually means something annoying to deal with. This one is simple enough, and I tap out a quick reply. *Yes, the guest list is in the file. I uploaded it two weeks ago.*

Ryan pulls up next to me and we both step out into the wind. Cheryl gave me a key, so I dash to the front door and unlock it. We duck inside.

"The weather is definitely not on our side today," Ryan says. He's wearing another perfectly fitting pair of jeans and a long sleeve t-shirt.

"No, it isn't. I haven't been to this event in years. Is it supposed to be outdoors?"

"Yeah, it starts here, and then there will be a line of canopies from here to the main plaza, all with artists displaying their work."

Lovely. One more wild card to account for in my plans: weather contingencies. I look around the gallery and wrinkle my nose.

"What's wrong?"

"I didn't realize the gallery was so run down." I flip a light switch, but it doesn't help much. The place is clean; I have to give it that. Not a speck of dust. The paintings and sculpture on display are nice enough, but the light is too dim, the floor has seen better days, and there's a large yellow spot on the ceiling where there was once a leak.

"It could use some restoration, but it's not so bad." Ryan's phone rings and he pulls it out of his back pocket and looks at the screen. "Sorry, one second. Hi, Mom."

I can hear his mother's muffled voice on the other end. I wander farther into the gallery so it doesn't seem like I'm eavesdropping. There's a haphazard mix of styles, not in any order that I can see. A few pieces of traditional Native American art are right next to an oil painting of a sunset on the beach. There are pedestals displaying sculpture, but they don't appear to be by the same artist, or even in the same style. A rack of postcards stands in the center of the room, right in the midst of everything.

"Yes, Mom," Ryan says. "I know. Okay, sure, I'll swing by later. No, it's no problem. Love you, too." He taps the screen and puts his phone back in his pocket. "Sorry."

"No, don't worry about it. How's your mom?"

"She's fine." He rubs the back of his neck. "She, um, she calls me a lot."

My mouth drops open a little and I swear my heart literally melts inside my chest. It isn't what Ryan said, but how he said it. He has this sweet, almost apologetic smile, and his tone is so ... protective.

"That's nice. She probably missed having you around.

She must have been ecstatic when you moved back to the beach."

"You have no idea. I crashed at my parents' house when I first got into town, and it took all of twenty-four hours for her to try to convince her neighbors to move so I could buy the house next door."

I laugh. I remember Mrs. Jacobsen as a sweet lady who talks a lot. I can just imagine her knocking on her neighbor's door, offering to have her son buy the place. "Something you probably found out about later."

"Exactly."

"Sort of how we ended up here?"

"Oh, you mean you didn't volunteer for this out of the goodness of your heart?"

I laugh again. "Not quite. My mom likes to volunteer me for things."

"You got voluntold too?"

"Yes!" Oh my god, he used my word. "She swears that isn't a word, but I'm pretty sure in the dictionary under voluntold, there's a picture of my mom with *that look* on her face."

"What, this one?" Ryan widens his eyes and plasters on an exaggerated smile. "But honey, this will be a great opportunity," he says in a high-pitched voice. "Besides, it means so much to the community."

I cover my mouth, laughing so hard my shoulders shake. "Were you in my kitchen the other day? Because that is my mom, spot on. Just add a little bit of barely concealed judgment and you've got it."

"I get that, too," he says and his smile fades a little.

I want to ask what he means, but the look on his face holds me back. "So what's it like, coming back here after ... where did you live before?"

"L.A. Honestly, I left Jetty Beach thinking I'd never come

back, except to visit my parents once in a while. This place seemed so small and backward." He shrugs again, the little line between his eyes standing out. That look is adorable. "Turns out city life wasn't what I thought it would be."

There's something behind his eyes, a pain I can almost feel. It makes me want to press myself against him and soothe all his hurts, whatever they are.

"And you're happier here?" I realize there's too much skepticism in my voice because a flash of defensiveness crosses his face. Damn it, I didn't mean to insult him. Again.

"A lot, actually."

My phone rings. I think about ignoring it, but it *is* business hours and technically, I am supposed to be working. "Sorry, it's my boss." I tap the screen to answer. "Hi Sandra."

"Nicole, where did you put the box of menus for the luncheon?" She sounds annoyed.

"They're in the workroom, on the bottom shelf. Right next to the copier."

"Oh. Right. Here they are. Thanks."

She hangs up without saying goodbye.

I let out a heavy sigh.

"Work issues?" Ryan asks.

"Sort of. Nothing major."

"So you're, what, working remotely? How does that work?"

Not very well, as it turns out. "Well, keeping up on emails and everything is easy enough. It wouldn't work long-term, but most of what I do, outside of an actual event day, is in the office. I spend the majority of my time coordinating with vendors and keeping track of details. I can do those things from anywhere."

"What exactly do you do?"

"We do event planning and PR stuff mostly."

"Do you like your job?"

Such an innocent, reasonable question. Yet it sends a surge of fear worming its way through my belly. Of course I like my job. It makes me look properly successful. My new title will look fabulous on my resume. But I still don't believe my own words when I say, "Yeah, I love my job. It's an amazing opportunity."

I'm not sure if Ryan believes me either.

"Why are we having the festival here, anyway?" I ask, wanting to change the subject. "This place is a mess. Maybe with some funding it could be nice again. But it's so dingy and sad. An art festival is supposed to be lively and full of energy."

"Sure, but it's tradition. This is like, the hub of Jetty Beach's art scene."

"Art scene? This is Jetty Beach, not some hip city with an artist's quarter."

"I know, it isn't much. But the locals love this place, and so do visitors. It's quirky."

I put my hands on my hips and look around again. Okay, he has a point. It is quirky.

"No one is really running the gallery right now, so I think we can make a few changes," he says. "We could move things around, maybe even put a fresh coat of paint on the walls. And I have some lighting that will help a lot. It's too dim in here, and so much of displaying a piece of art is getting the lighting right."

I'm a little skeptical, but Ryan sounds like he knows what he's doing. "All right, I suppose we can try to spruce the place up a bit."

"I have the lights up at my place. If you want to follow me out there, I could give them to you."

I blink in surprise. Strictly speaking, we don't need the

lights today. Ryan can bring them the next time he comes into town. But for reasons I cannot fathom, I find myself saying, "Sure, that sounds great," before I have a chance to even think.

He looks a little stunned himself. Is he surprised I said yes, or surprised he just asked me to come to his house? I follow him outside into the wind. The rain has slacked off a little, but my hair blows around my face. I get into my car and try to smooth it down, but it isn't going to cooperate. I grab a clip from my purse, twist my hair, and pin it up. Ryan glances over at me from the driver's seat of his car. I nod and give him a thumbs up.

Oh my god, Nicole, what was that? I'm such a dork.

I follow him through the town entrance, to the highway that leads north. My heart beats a little too quickly and butterflies dance in my belly.

This is fine. Today wasn't a date, and he isn't inviting you up to his place. You're just going to pick up some lights.

I'm not sure if I want that to be true, or not.

7

NICOLE

The old church is set well away from the road, down a long gravel driveway. I can hear the waves crashing as soon as I open the car door. The building itself is weathered gray with white trim. A covered front porch leads to double doors in front, and the roof slopes to a high peak in the center. There's no longer a cross or any sort of religious adornment on the outside. It hasn't been used as a church since well before my lifetime. Yet it still retains its character, a quaintness that speaks of a simpler time.

Ryan gets out of his car and pauses, looking up at the old building. He clearly has an affection for the place—the half-smile on his face tells me that. The wind blows, chilling me to the bone. It's cold this close to the beach. I wrap my cardigan tighter and follow Ryan to the front door.

"Well, this is it," he says, ushering me in.

Light streams in through tall windows with detailed wood trim. Their pointed tops make them almost look medieval, at least to my eyes. Hardwood floors gleam and the room is filled with a haphazard arrangement of furniture. A burgundy velvet chaise sits next to a lush leather armchair. A tall, freestanding mirror with a dark wood frame stands near a cream-colored couch accented with blue throw pillows.

There are a few side tables that look like refinished antiques, and a number of decorative pots and urns, but none of it seems to be placed in any sort of order. Along the walls, large sheets of beige canvas cover what appears to be more furniture. Photographer's lights and black umbrellas with reflective white centers, all mounted on stands, crowd around the jumbled display.

"Sorry," Ryan says. "I was moving things around after my last shoot, so the studio is a mess."

"That's okay. It's beautiful."

He looks around, a proud smile on his face. "Thanks. It was a disaster when I bought it. You wouldn't have recognized it. There were holes in the walls, and the floor looked terrible. It's taken a lot of work, but it's definitely come together."

I wander over to one of the windows. It reveals a breathtaking view of the beach. The church sits on a bluff overlooking the ocean. Rolling dunes peppered with tall grasses give way to the gray sand of the beach, stretching in both directions. Waves crash against the sand, foamy white water rolling back and forth in a steady rhythm.

"This is amazing."

Ryan moves in behind me, his closeness making my back tingle. "Yeah, the view is incredible. It's almost as good as the lighting in here."

I stand, rooted to the spot, suddenly afraid to turn around. Ryan is so close I can smell him. His scent is fresh and clean, like a breeze blowing through the woods on a spring day. Jason took to wearing cologne. My stomach turns a little as I think about it. He was probably trying to mask the smell of the other woman's perfume. I push that out of my mind and take a deep breath, filling my lungs with Ryan's scent.

My heart thunders in my chest. I'm sure he can hear it. I turn, suddenly desperate for something to break the tension.

Boobs catch my eye.

Well, doesn't that just break the spell?

The walls on either side of the front door are lined with framed photographs. The first one I notice has a woman in a vintage-style bikini, her boobs barely contained by navy and white polka-dots. Her hair and makeup are done pinup style, like someone from the forties. I walk across the room to get a closer look. She's leaning against the hood of an old car, her back arched, legs a mile long ending in red stilettos.

"Wow," I say. "Did you take this?"

"I did."

I glance at the other photographs. They're all scantily clad women in various provocative poses. Another looks kind of vintage like the first one, the girl in a sexy version of a sailor outfit, complete with a little cap on her head. A more modern-looking woman looks backward over her shoulder, the lines of her waist extending to lush hips, her body only covered by a thin wisp of fabric she holds up with one hand. The light is soft against her olive skin, and her hair hangs down over her shoulder in gentle waves.

A third is of a woman lying on the burgundy velvet chaise I noticed in the studio. Somehow she makes the long sequined gown she's wearing look more erotic than the bikinis and lingerie on the women in the other photos. Her arm drapes carelessly over her forehead and her other hand teases near her groin. Voluminous auburn hair spreads out over the back of the chaise, and her red lips stand out against pale skin.

"These are gorgeous," I say, and I mean it. I was taken aback at first, but there's nothing trashy about these photos. They're sexual, sure, but in a way that's sensual rather than raunchy.

"You like them?" He stands with his hands in his pockets, his head tilted just a bit to the right. His eyes meet mine. "I was a little worried."

"Why?"

He shrugs. "Not everyone understands what I do."

"Is this, um..." I pause, not quite sure how to phrase my question. "Is this the type of photography you do?"

"Mostly, yeah. I've done lingerie lines, and a lot of portfolio shots for models. I also do private boudoir sessions."

"Boudoir? Like, sexy photos women give their husbands?"

"Exactly. Do you ... do you want to see some?"

"Sure."

He brings out a thick leather-bound book and nods toward the couch. I sit down next to him and he opens the book in his lap. The first photo is a woman splayed out on a bed, wearing nothing but a white sheet. Her skin looks flawless, but she isn't covered in tons of makeup. Thick, blond hair flows out behind her, and the whole thing looks ... it looks gorgeous. Like the photos on his wall, it's highly charged with sexuality, but not the least bit trashy.

He slowly flips through more pages. Some women wear lingerie, others appear to be nude, strategically covered by a sheet. They are of varying ages. One woman is silver-haired, with wrinkles and folds in her skin, but he made her look just as sensual as the younger women.

"This isn't what I was thinking when you said boudoir

photos," I say, lingering over a photograph of a woman in a man's shirt and tie. "I would never have guessed they could be so classy. You've even done some in black and white. These are incredible."

"You were picturing red and black corsets with lots of lace and bad makeup?"

"Yeah, kinda. Probably not fair of me, but I've never seen anyone's boudoir photos before."

He turns the page again, this time to a woman in a black teddy. It could be in a catalog. "I get paid a lot more to shoot models, but these are my favorite shoots by far. I love helping women bring out their inner goddess."

"Wow, you definitely deliver," I say, trying to keep my voice from sounding breathy. "How did you get into doing this? Did you just wake up one day and think, hey, I'd like to take photos of half-naked women and make them look like goddesses?"

Ryan chuckles. "Not quite. I went to art school and spent a lot of time taking pictures of trees and farmland and stuff. There's a lot of beauty in nature, but I've always been drawn to people. Well, women in particular. After graduating I did a stint taking photos for a ... certain kind of website."

"Porn?"

"Yeah, it was definitely porn. Really raunchy stuff, but it paid the bills."

I'm not quite sure what to make of that. What must his family think? If he even told them. "That must have been ... interesting."

"You'd think it would be the perfect gig for a twenty-two-year-old guy, but honestly, it was awful. There was no emotion in any of it. Just ... hell, I don't even want to tell you. Let's just say I saw things that year that I will never be able to unsee."

"So you weren't bringing home your subjects and acting out the photos?" I nudge him with my elbow.

"No," he says with a laugh, and stands up. He puts the book back on a shelf. "No, I got out of that job as soon as I could. Sometimes I feel like all the showers in the world won't be enough to wash off the ick."

"How did you go from porn to, well, sexy but not porn?"

One side of his mouth turns up in a grin. "Luck, mostly. I took a job as a janitor at this old mansion just to keep a roof over my head. It used to be someone's home, but now it's rented out for weddings and stuff. One day this well-known photographer came in to scout out the space for a shoot. I was just leaving from working all night, but I recognized him and worked up the nerve to introduce myself. I ended up showing him around the grounds—pointed out all the best places to shoot, and where the sun would be at different times of day and so forth. I guess he was impressed because he started hiring me to help with some of his clients. He taught me a lot. I found I had a good eye for women's bodies—for capturing their sensuality. Eventually clients started asking for me specifically. I contracted out to some ad agencies and designers, and built up a client list."

"And now you're here. This is a far cry from L.A."

"Thank goodness for that. Fortunately, a lot of my clients are willing to come here for me to shoot them. That's why I bought the church. The unique architecture is a selling point. My clients love it. Plus, I can travel when I need to."

I want to ask him why he moved back to the beach. It seems like he had a promising career. What would have brought him back here?

"So, the lights are over here," Ryan says, before I can ask any more questions.

I glance one more time at Ryan's photos, imagining him

talking the women through their photo shoots. How did he get them to look so ... stirring? The woman on the chaise looks like she might be getting ready to have an orgasm. She doesn't have an exaggerated *oh-baby-do-it-now* face—she looks relaxed, her eyelids fluttering closed, her lips parted, like she's experiencing sublime bliss. Did Ryan do that? Or is she simply an experienced model who knows how to put on the right expression?

I've never been a switch hitter, but the woman's expression and the languid drape of her arms makes my heart beat faster. I tear my gaze away, not wanting to make my face turn red. It's probably too late for that. Thankfully Ryan's studio is chilly, or it would be worse. I follow him through a doorway on the other side of the room, resisting the urge to fan myself as I walk.

A rectangular room, clearly his living space, opens up. The ceiling is high, but flat instead of pitched. Another window has an equally spectacular view of the beach. There's a little kitchen area along one side, and he has a couch and armchair facing a TV mounted to the wall. But the bulk of the room is dominated by a king-size bed. In true guy fashion, it's plain, with just a green comforter and a couple of pillows, all slightly askew.

I arch an eyebrow as I look at the bed. "What family do you share that with?"

His eyes dart to the bed and he gives me that lopsided smile again. For half a second, I imagine lying in the center of that huge bed, Ryan crawling on top of me.

"I like my space when I sleep."

I clear my throat, suddenly wishing I hadn't called attention to the bed.

Ryan grabs what looks like a black suitcase. "These are

the lights. They're similar to the ones out in the studio, but they're portable."

"Great, that will be perfect."

He hesitates, his eyes on my face. A tingle runs down my spine.

Suddenly even more conscious of the bed, I duck through the doorway back into the studio. My brain tells me to head for the front door, but I move to one of the windows instead. What am I doing, lingering here?

I hear him set down the black case, and he moves to stand behind me.

"Beautiful." His voice is quiet—soft and low.

"It is. I can see why you wanted this place."

"Mm hmm." He murmurs something I can't quite make out.

I turn to ask him what he said, but he's standing so close, the words flee before I can speak. His gaze is intense, and the line between his eyes furrows.

My heart flutters and my stomach does a little somersault. I tilt my chin up and part my lips. He leans in, almost imperceptibly, the intensity never leaving his expression. I draw in a quick breath, waiting, my body coming alive. I'm stuck, frozen, the rest of the world ceasing to exist. There's nothing but his eyes on my face, piercing and eager.

The front door flies open. "Hey, you home?"

Ryan steps back and I feel blood rush to my face.

"Don't you knock?" Ryan asks.

Ryan's older brother Cody walks in, shutting the door behind him. "Sorry, man, I didn't know you had company."

"The other car in the driveway wasn't a clue?" Ryan asks.

I blink hard and take a deep breath, hoping I don't look as stunned as I feel. What just happened?

"Cody, you remember Nicole Prescott?" Ryan says, gesturing to me.

"Yeah, sure," Cody says, walking over to shake my hand. The family resemblance is obvious. He has the same dark hair and green eyes, although his is cut shorter. He wears a light green button-down shirt, striped tie, and a pair of dark slacks. "You're from Jetty Beach, right? In Ryan's class? That's crazy, I can't remember the last time I saw you."

I shake Cody's hand. He takes it in a firm grip. "Yeah, I haven't been back in a while."

"Are you back for good?" Cody asks.

"No," I say. Did Ryan flinch when I said that? "I'm just here temporarily, while I take care of some things."

"Nice. Hey, sorry to interrupt. Ryan, you should answer mom's text."

"Mom texted?" Ryan asks, a look of amusement on his face.

"She most certainly did," Cody says. "Of course, you didn't answer, and now she wants to know why."

"Did you come all the way up here to find out why I didn't answer a text from someone who has literally never texted me before in her entire life?"

Cody shrugs. "That's not the only reason. Mom wants us all over for dinner."

"We have dinner there every week," Ryan says. "Why does this one need a special invite?"

"Mom was really adamant about it," Cody says. "Have you heard from Hunter recently?"

I vaguely remember Hunter. He wasn't Ryan and Cody's brother, but it seems like he was always with the Jacobsens. Maybe he even lived with them.

"No, I never hear from him," Ryan says. "Why? Do you think this is about him?"

"Maybe," Cody says. "Mom was acting weird, made me wonder. You know how she is when she's trying to hide something from us. I thought maybe you heard something."

"No, but you can tell Mom I'll be at dinner," Ryan says. "I'll text her. And you could have just called me."

Cody leans against a little table next to the door. "I know, but I was out and about."

Confusion swirls in my mind. Had Ryan been about to kiss me? Did I want him to? I mean, yes, I wanted him to. There's a part of me that wants to launch myself at him, put my hands all over that amazing body. Let him put his hands all over mine. But what does that make me? I just got out of the only relationship I've ever been in. Jumping into bed with a guy I barely know is definitely a terrible idea.

Isn't it?

I pick up the black case and nod toward the door. "I should probably get back."

"Hey, don't leave on my account," Cody says.

"No, no, you're fine. I was just picking up some lights." I lift the case a little. "I'll see you later, Ryan."

Ryan runs a hand through his hair. "Yeah. I'll probably talk to you tomorrow."

I feel as if I'm walking through a dream as I cross the studio to the front door. Ryan jogs a few steps to get in front of me and holds the door open. "Do you need any help with that?"

"No, it's not heavy. I'll just put it in the back seat."

"Okay. Thanks for coming by."

He meets my eyes for a second. My body screams for him to touch me. A quick hug, a hand on my arm, anything to give me a clue as to whether that moment in his studio had been real.

His brow furrows again and he steps away, his arm

extending to hold the door open. I walk out toward my car and hear the door close behind me. I tell myself not to look back. I want so badly to see him standing there, the closed door between us and his brother for one more minute of privacy. Glancing over my shoulder, I feel my heart sink. He's inside.

I blow out a breath, wanting to kick myself for being such an idiot, and put the lights in the car. It's been so long since I've been single, my radar is completely off. He was probably just looking at the view. Sure, he was friendly, but he wasn't flirting. Not really.

Do I even know what flirting looks like anymore?

I get into my car and drive down the long driveway, telling myself in a very stern voice that I am imagining things. Nothing happened. Ryan isn't even into me.

8
RYAN

I close the door, hesitating with my hand on the dead bolt. I want to go back out there, shut the door behind me, and have a few minutes of privacy with her. Actually, I want a lot more than that. Her scent is so intoxicating; my head is still swimming with it.

Of course, it's likely I imagined the whole thing. She could have been looking at the view. Nicole probably isn't even into me.

She shouldn't be into me. I'm not any good for her.

"Hey, sorry man, did I interrupt something?" Cody asks.

"It's no big deal." I shrug. "She was just here to pick up those lights."

Cody heads through the studio into my apartment. "Got any beer?"

"Yeah." I take a second to collect myself, hoping the raging hard-on I'm sporting will go down quickly. What is it about Nicole? Just looking at her makes me feel like a fucking teenager. Zero control. When Cody showed up I was two seconds from grabbing her, running my hands all over that hot body, devouring her with my mouth. Would she have let me?

Cody comes back out to the studio, two beers in his hands. He hands one to me. "Sorry for the cock block, man."

"Nah, it was nothing like that."

Cody raises an eyebrow. "Your little buddy there thinks otherwise."

"Fuck off and quit looking at my dick."

Cody laughs and takes a swig of his beer. "So what do you think's going on with Mom?"

"I don't know. I just saw her a few days ago and she seemed fine. Do you think it's really Hunter?"

Hunter is the youngest Jacobsen brother in all but name. His dad left when he was just a baby and his mom did the best she could, but it was tough for a single mother. Hunter didn't exactly make it easy on her. My parents stepped in and took care of him a lot of the time, giving his poor mom a break. A few years later, his mom died and Hunter lived with us from then on.

Until he up and left, that is.

"It might be Hunter," Cody says. "It would be like Mom to try to surprise us."

I'm not sure how I feel about that. I'm still pissed at Hunter for leaving the way he did. I take a long pull from the bottle, distracted by my cock. It is not cooperating. I wish Cody would go, so I could take care of it. With thoughts of Nicole still lingering, it's going to take no time at all to get myself off. Maybe the release will calm me down. I hope so. Something needs to.

Cody wanders back into the apartment. "Got anything to eat?"

I roll my eyes and follow him in. My brother and I get

along pretty well, but he's irritating the shit out of me right now. "Don't you have somewhere to be?"

"Nope. They kicked me out of the clinic after my last patient. Said I've been working too much."

Cody's a doctor. Because of course he is. My parents love to introduce their son, Dr. Jacobsen, to people. To be fair, he's a great doctor. He's always been smart, and even though he tends to annoy the crap out of me, he's good with people. Personable. Probably has a great bedside manner.

"What about Jennifer?" I ask.

"What about her?"

"I don't know, maybe you're seeing her or something. Isn't she your girlfriend? I thought it was customary for guys to spend time with their girlfriends."

Cody lets out a breath, his beer dangling between his fingers. "Things are kind of shitty with us lately."

"That sucks."

"Yeah. It does."

"Did you actually break up, or are you just fighting again?"

"Honestly, I'm not even sure this time. I haven't talked to her in a couple of days."

I hope this might be it for Cody and Jennifer. On the surface, she seems perfect for Cody. Successful in her own right, she owns a boutique clothing store in town. She owns her condo on the beach, drives a nice car. She certainly isn't using Cody for his doctor's income.

But the fact that she isn't a gold digger is more or less the only thing in her favor. I suppose men find her attractive, but I can't see past the resting bitch face. As far as I'm concerned, she's selfish and demanding, and Cody can do better. I have no idea why he keeps going back to her. They've been on again, off again for a couple of years.

"Well, maybe it's time to move on or whatever. You guys are always fighting about something."

"I know," Cody says. He drains the last of his beer and sets the bottle on the counter. His brow furrows, and he walks over to my dresser. "Don't you open your mail? This thing has been sitting here forever."

"Leave it."

"What, am I a dog now?" Cody asks with a laugh. "Oh shit, is this from Ohio?"

"Yes."

"Is it from Elise's family?"

I walk over to the dresser and turn the letter over, hiding the return address. "Forget about it."

Cody glances away. "All right, man. Just, if you open it, and it triggers something ... call me, okay?"

"Yeah, whatever. Just leave it alone."

"Really, Ryan, I don't want—"

"I'm fine, Cody."

"No bullshit?"

"No bullshit."

"Okay. Good. I'll get out of here, then. I should run to the store. I don't think there's any food in my house."

He leaves through the studio, and I wait until I hear the crunch of gravel under his tires as he drives away. I glance at the letter, leaving it turned over. Just touching it makes me nervous. It's a part of my past I'm not ready to face. I don't know if I ever will be, yet I leave it sitting out, like I need the reminder.

My erection is half-gone. Thinking about Jennifer has that effect on me—yet another reason I can't understand why Cody is with her. The thought of trying to fuck that woman. *Ugh.* I shudder.

I walk over to the window and take another sip, resting

my other arm against the molding. Thick clouds hide the sun, but I can tell it's sinking toward the water. The horizon has a soft pink and orange cast to it. Certainly not the most brilliant sunset I've ever seen, but it has good composition. Subtle.

Nicole. Thoughts of her come to me unbidden, and I'm instantly hard again. Why does she do that to me? I think about the way she looked, standing in front of the windows in the studio. The light playing off her hair, highlighting the little loose strands around her neck. I was standing behind her, close enough to touch her. Smell her.

Fuck it, I'm doing this. I strip down and get into the shower. The hot water patters against me and I run my hands over my head, wetting my hair. My cock is still hard, so I grab it and stroke the swollen flesh. I imagine Nicole, her tight ass lifted up for me, her head turned so I can see her face. I'd pound into her, hard and fast. She'd beg me to keep going, but I'd slow down, teasing her, making her wait. The intensity builds and I stroke faster. Nicole straddled over the top of me, my hands on her breasts. She'd grind her pussy into me and—

The orgasm hits me in a rush. Shit, that's a good one. The tension eases as I come. After I finish, I stand with my hands against the tiles, breathing hard.

I haven't wanted a woman like this in a long time. Truth be told, I haven't wanted a woman at all in a long time. Not since Elise. Since I moved home, I've been avoiding connecting with anyone. I'm still too raw. Opening myself up to someone else is dangerous. I know I run the risk of sinking back into the dismal pit of depression, and if I do, I'm not sure if I'm strong enough to claw my way back out.

But I'm not sure I'm strong enough to keep my distance from Nicole, either.

9

NICOLE

The next few days go by in a blur. Keeping up with work grows more difficult. I know I need to get back in the office, but I'm not sure I can face it yet. There's still a framed picture of me and Jason on my desk. Everyone in the office will know by now what happened. What must they think? Amy in Accounting shamelessly flirted with Jason at the last holiday party. Is she gloating? My flight back to Jetty Beach probably made it worse. I must look like such a weakling, running off to my parents' house just because of a stupid breakup. Who does that?

I sit at the island in my parents' kitchen, trying to get some work done, but my mind isn't cooperating. My eyes drift to the black case sitting near the front door. I haven't seen Ryan since I picked up the lights at his house. There hasn't been a reason for us to get together. More than once, I've found myself trying to come up with an excuse to text him. There has to be festival business to take care of, right? That's all it is. We have a lot of work to do.

Ryan seems like a good guy—he deserves better than being my rebound. I can't seem to get him out of my head, but it's because I'm lonely. I was with Jason too long. I need to spend some time as me, get to know who I am without being a part of a relationship. I hardly know what that's like.

So far? *Lonely*. That's what it's like.

Melissa calls and invites me out to lunch. I run a brush through my hair and throw on a fluttery blue blouse and a pair of slacks, dressing it down with sandals instead of heels. Her car is already outside the fish and chips place she picked, so I go inside, finding her at a window booth.

"Hey." I slide into the seat and put my purse next to me. Two ice waters sit on the table. "I'm glad you called. I think I needed to get out of the house."

"I figured." Her hair is swept up in a ponytail and she's wearing her old Rolling Stones t-shirt.

"Wait, isn't it like, a Wednesday? Why aren't you at work?"

"Half day. I should probably be grading projects, but I'm kind of over it right now. I'll catch up this weekend. So, what's going on with you?"

"Nothing." She gives me her *I'm not buying it* look. "Okay, not nothing. This art festival is going to be a disaster, and the whole town will be there to see it. Not to mention, my boss is sending me passive-aggressive emails about work. If she needs me back in the office, I wish she would just say so."

The corner of Melissa's lip turns up in a half-smile. "That's not what I meant."

"What did you mean, then?" I ask, not bothering to keep the exasperation out of my voice.

"I know you're stressed about work, and the festival and all that. But there's something else. I can tell."

"What on earth are you talking about?"

"See? There it is," she says, pointing at my face, her tone

triumphant.

"Where?" I look over my shoulder. "There what is?"

"You're already blushing."

"I am not!"

"You definitely are. Nic, I know you. I've known you since we were kids. I don't know why you think you can hide anything from me."

I lick my lips, willing the memory of Ryan's face drawing closer to mine out of my head. My cheeks warm, and I know I'm getting flushed.

"Tell me."

"Honestly, it was nothing," I say, and it's not even a lie. "Nothing happened."

"Whoa, honey. *Nothing happened* means something might have happened. Or could have happened. Or *almost* happened. So what was it that didn't happen?"

I take a drink of my water, trying to gather my thoughts. "I went out to Ryan's place the other day."

"Ryan Jacobsen? Wait, you need to back up. Why did you go to Ryan's place?"

"He's on the festival committee. Actually, he and I *are* the festival committee. So anyway, he brought me to his house."

"Ooh," Melissa says, waggling her eyebrows.

"Shut it, Simon. Like I said, nothing actually happened. I went with him to pick up some lights to take to the gallery."

"But?"

"But ... I don't know. I was looking out at the view—which is incredible, by the way—and he was standing behind me. I turned around and ... he was right there, so close. He was staring at me with this super intense look on his face."

"And?"

"Well, I think he might have been moving in to kiss me,

but his brother showed up."

"Cody?"

"Yep. Walked right in and that was it."

"Oh my god. You had an *almost*."

"An *almost*? What does that even mean?"

"You know, that moment when two people who really want to kiss each other almost do, but then they're interrupted," she says, like I should know. She grins at me again. "What would you have done if Cody hadn't shown up?"

I sigh, looking off through the window behind Melissa. "Let's just say it's probably a good thing Cody came. I must have been losing my mind."

She leans over the table. "You wanted him."

"Shut up." I toss a napkin at her.

"You totally did. Fuck it, Nicole. You should hit that."

"Did you really just say 'hit that'?"

"I did, and I mean it. Let's be honest here, Ryan is massively hot."

I raise my eyebrows at her, but my unspoken protest is total bullshit and we both know it. He is massively hot.

"Stop overthinking it. You're into him, and I'd bet money he's into you."

"He probably isn't."

She rolls her eyes. "Really? Come on, Nicole. You might have been off the market for a long time, but you're not an idiot. Why is he on the festival committee again? I'm betting it isn't because he's passionate about art."

"He is passionate about art, as a matter of fact. He's a photographer. But that's beside the point. You're right about me being off the market. I was never really on the market. I got together with Jason when we were seventeen. He's the only guy I've ever been with. I don't know anything about dating. Not really."

Melissa taps her chin. "Well, the important thing is to start this on the right foot. How are you looking down below?" She raises an eyebrow and points her finger downward.

"Down below? Are you serious?"

"I'm completely serious. You can't have another *almost* that turns into *oh-my-god-Ryan-take-me-now* if you aren't properly groomed."

I gape at her.

"You know what, you were right. It *is* good that Cody showed up and ruined your moment. Now we have time to get you ready."

"I don't need you to get me ready."

Melissa raises an eyebrow. "Oh really? Have you even shaved your legs once since you've been here?"

"Um—"

She grabs her purse and stands. "Come on. We'll eat later."

"Where are we going?"

"Field trip."

JOSIE'S NAILS sits at the end of a long row of shops. A gaudy neon sign in the window proclaims *Manicures! Pedicures! Waxing!* and poster of a woman with slick red nails is taped to the door.

I stop outside. "Wait."

"What's the problem?" Melissa asks, her hand on the door handle.

"I don't think I want to do this."

"No way. You're not changing your mind now." She grabs my hand and pulls me toward the door.

"I never actually agreed to anything. You didn't give me a chance."

"Stop being a baby."

"I'm not being a baby. Couldn't we at least drive a few towns away to do this? I don't think I want Josie seeing my lady parts. I know her. She knows my mom."

Melissa laughs. "She's really good. Promise."

"She might be the best waxer in the state, but she'll ask questions. What am I supposed to tell her if she asks why I'm doing this? Nothing is actually happening with Ryan. I don't want Josie talking, and word spreading that we're sleeping together or something."

"Believe it or not, Josie is very discreet. Trust me."

I bite my lower lip, but stop protesting and follow her inside.

"Hey, Josie," Melissa says.

"Hey, sweetie." Josie has bleached-blond hair that she wears with her bangs teased up like it's 1982. Blue eyeliner, light denim jeans, and a slouchy pink shirt complete her endearing, if dated, look. "Having a ladies' day out? How about mani-pedis for the both of you?"

"Actually, Nicole here is in need of some grooming of the delicate variety," Melissa says, tossing a wink in my direction.

"Ah," Josie says, with a knowing arch of her eyebrow. "This way."

Josie leads me to a back room with an upholstered table. The walls are painted pale blue and a little fountain trickles in the corner. It's probably meant to be soothing, but it makes me suddenly terrified I'll have to pee in the middle of this insanity.

"Um, I've never done this before," I say.

"A virgin, huh." Her bright pink nails click as she busies

herself with something on a side counter. "Don't worry. I've done this a million times. It's not nearly as bad as you'd think."

I stand near the door, feeling awkward, half wishing Melissa came in with me, and half glad she didn't. What am I supposed to do? Get naked? Take off all my clothes, or just my pants? I showered earlier, but maybe I should have gone home and showered again, so I'd be fresh.

Josie turns, an empty shot glass in her hand. "Whiskey or tequila?"

"You give your clients shots before you wax them?"

"It will help you relax."

This is such a bad idea. "Whiskey."

The bottle clinks as Josie pours. "Good choice. Most girls your age seem to think the definition of a shot is tequila. That's why I started keeping it around. But a good whiskey..." She pauses, handing me the glass. "Doesn't even have to be expensive. This one's nice and smooth. Goes down easy."

I tilt my head back and swallow. She's right, it is smooth. It burns down my throat, but in seconds I feel the warmth spreading.

"Okay, Josie," I say, mustering what little courage I can, "let's do this."

"All right, I need you up on the table, Winnie-the-Pooh style."

Winnie-the? "What?"

"No bottoms," she says. "You can keep your top on."

My face warms. "Oh, right."

I hesitate, waiting for Josie to leave so I can undress. She keeps her back to me, but makes no move to go. Feeling enormously awkward, I undress. I fold my jeans and tuck my panties inside, out of sight. That makes me feel like a bigger idiot. Josie is about to get real acquainted with my lady parts—she isn't going to flinch at seeing a scrap of pink cotton.

I lay down, feeling more exposed than I do at the gynecologist. At least then they give you that big blue paper to cover up with. I tug on my shirt, hoping to decrease the amount of skin showing. My face is on fire. Should I have trimmed first? This is ridiculous.

"Okay, sweetie," Josie says, her tone suddenly soft and soothing, "you just look up at the ceiling and don't worry a bit about what I'm doing."

Don't worry? She has to be kidding. Josie takes one leg and bends it, then tips it outward, putting my legs into a sort of flamingo pose. I swear there's a breeze. I dig my teeth into my lower lip and squeeze my eyes shut while she spreads the warm wax.

"Do you want to leave a little in the front?" she asks. "How does he like it?"

"Oh, no, there's no *he*. I'm just ... I don't know what I'm doing."

"Hmm," Josie says, still working. "How do you want it, then? Landing strip, triangle, or totally smooth?"

I figure if I leave some in front, there will be less wax. "Triangle."

Josie's hands press against me. I'm too terrified to look.

"And, go."

For half a second, I almost think it doesn't hurt. Then the pain hits me. Despite myself, I shriek and clap my hands over my mouth. It feels like she tore the skin right off.

My scream doesn't faze Josie. She pushes my legs apart, despite my attempts to clamp my knees together, and applies more wax.

Oh fuck, she's going to do it again.

"And, go."

My hands still cover my mouth and I keep from squealing, but only just. The skin burns like hell. I am going to kill Melissa.

"You're doing great," Josie says.

"You're full of shit."

Josie laughs and moves my knee higher.

Ten minutes later, I have tears leaking out of my eyes, but Josie kept going, and I didn't die. I start to feel a little proud of myself. I'm going to make it.

"Okay, sweetie, now I need to do your labia," Josie says. "That area is pretty sensitive, but I'll do my best to be gentle."

I whimper as I feel Josie's fingers touch me along the soft folds of skin between my legs. This is absolutely insane. This is—

"Fuck!"

"There you go," Josie says. "Let it out."

She pulls again and I let the f-bombs fly. This has to end soon. I think about telling her to stop, but I know I'll never let her start again. Then what will I do? A half-waxed pussy is probably worse than what I had before.

Josie goes back to the counter, leaving me with my legs splayed wide, my lady garden throbbing. I want to reach down and grab myself, but I'm afraid to touch it. I take a few deep breaths. Did I really do it? I did. I survived my first waxing.

"Time to turn over," she says. "On your side, please."

"What?"

"We can't leave the back end fuzzy," she says, as if this is the most obvious thing in the world.

Torn between hysterical laughter and sobbing like a baby, I turn.

"Spread your cheeks, please."

Oh, you have got to be kidding me.

I do as she asks, pulling apart my ass cheeks. Josie pokes, presses, and pulls. I squeeze my eyes shut and smoosh my forehead into the table to keep from crying out again.

After what feels like an eternity, but is probably five more minutes, she's finished. She turns me over and slathers on something she says will help prevent ingrown hairs and speed healing. I stare at the ceiling, afraid to move.

Josie pats my arm. "You did great, sweetie. You can stay there for a few minutes. Get up when you're ready."

I mumble something as she leaves. Scrunching my nose and squeezing my eyes almost shut, I lift my head so I can see. She left a perfect triangle of dark blond hair and the skin on either side doesn't look too bad. It's red and maybe a little swollen—but as bad as it hurt, I expected worse.

Worse is between my legs.

I open my knees just a bit and gape in horror. My labia are huge. Thick and red, they look like I've been in a fight, using my vagina as my primary weapon.

Melissa is so dead.

I get up and dress, slipping my panties on gingerly. Slacks were the wrong thing to wear to my first waxing. They press against my newly shorn skin, reminding me how tender I am.

"There, isn't that better?" Melissa asks when I emerge from the back room. She gets up from the dryer chair she's been sitting in. "You okay?"

I glare at her.

"You'll thank me later," she says.

I pay the bill, finding it bizarre to tip a woman who just turned my hoo-ha into a throbbing mass of pain. With a glance over my shoulder to make sure Melissa isn't looking, I scrawl a quick note on the bottom of the receipt.

Next time Melissa Simon comes in – torture her.

10

NICOLE

*P*apers are scattered over the countertop. I groan, realizing my mug left a brown coffee ring on a manila file folder. Cheryl Johnson's organization system can only be described as nonexistent. She kept receipts from Old Town Café, but neglected to save copies of the festival permits or the sponsorship forms. I let out a heavy sigh and pinch the bridge of my nose.

My phone dings and I check my messages again. Another email from work. I made the commitment to help with the festival, but if people in my office don't start pulling their own weight, there's no way I can stay. Sandra is panicking over details again—details her own assistant is supposed to be handling. I fire off a terse email to her assistant, and cc Sandra. Maybe it's bad form to make it look like I'm throwing the assistant under the bus, but I feel like I'm ready to snap.

Bing. My phone again. I eye it with suspicion. Are they pissed at me now?

It's a text from Ryan. *What are you up to?*

My heart jumps and I chew on my lip before responding. *Going through Cheryl's paperwork. Nightmare.*

Sounds terrifying.

I laugh. *Scarier than a horror movie.*

There's a long pause. I hold my phone in my hands, staring at the screen, waiting for a reply. The screen goes dark and I put the phone down, way too disappointed. This is silly.

It *bings* again and I snatch it up, almost giddy with anticipation. What is he going to say next?

Another email. My shoulders slump.

There is definitely something wrong with me. I should be grieving. The end of a decade-long relationship ought to call for a period of mourning. I'm still hurt by what Jason did, but every time I think about Ryan, it hurts a little less. However, that's no excuse for acting like a twitterpated schoolgirl. What am I doing, bursting with anticipation over a stupid text message?

Bing. I force my hand to slow down and pick up my phone without so much enthusiasm.

Sorry. Cody being a dumbass. Typical. Are you hungry?

A smile breaks out over my face. So much for tempering my excitement. *Yeah, starving.*

Can I pick you up in 20?

Sounds great.

I blow out a breath and gather up the paperwork into a neat stack. Twenty minutes. A sudden rush of nervousness hits me and my stomach turns over. I think about the way he looked, standing so close to me near the windows in his studio. I can't get the *what if* out of my head.

It's okay Nicole. You've got this.

∼

NINETEEN MINUTES LATER—NOT that I'm counting—Ryan pulls up. My dad's home, tinkering in the shop out back, so I slip out the front door. I don't really want to answer awkward questions from my parents about where I'm going. It feels surreal, like I'm a kid sneaking out to meet a guy they don't like. Not that I ever dated someone they didn't like. I really only dated Jason, and everyone loved him.

The sight of Ryan stepping out of his car pushes all thoughts of Jason from my mind. He's dressed in a blue t-shirt and dark jeans. His hair looks wind-blown, like it always does, and his jaw is covered in just the right amount of stubble. What would that stubble feel like on my cheek? On my—

"Hey," he says. He walks around the other side of the car to open the door for me.

"Thanks."

He shuts the door and gets in on the driver's side. "I figured you were working. Thought you might be hungry."

"I really am. Come to think of it, I don't know if I've eaten since breakfast."

"You do that a lot, don't you?" he asks as he pulls out of the driveway.

"Do what?"

"Get so busy you don't take care of yourself."

I give him a sidelong glance and a small smile. "Maybe. So, what, we've worked together on this thing for a few days, and now you know all about me?"

He laughs. "Oh no. I'm not going there."

"Going where? You seem to have me all figured out. You knew I'd be hungry."

"Lucky guess. It's seven o'clock."

Suddenly I wonder why he invited me to dinner. Is this a date? Are we supposed to be working? I tuck my hair behind my ear and try to sneak a glance at him. He seems relaxed, but that could mean anything.

"Is pizza okay?" he asks.

"Roma's?" Roma's was one of the go-to Friday night hang outs when I was in high school. "Sure, I haven't been there in years."

"Neither have I. I thought it might be kinda fun to go."

We pull up to the red building and get out. It's a mild night—the wind from the past few days has blown itself out, and the sky is soft and turning purple.

Ryan holds the door for me, and it's like walking into the past. Everything is exactly the same. Low walls with rough wood paneling separate each booth, and patrons sit on red vinyl benches. The scents of garlic, oregano, and cheap beer mingle in the air. An alcove on one side has a line of ancient arcade games, their screens still blinking and colorful. The menu has all of five choices, the same as it always has. We order at the counter and take a plastic number sign to a booth near the back.

The walls are covered with years of graffiti—encouraged by the owners. Kids doodle, people sign their names, and the locals make a point of covering anything that looks like it's been written by tourists. In a town whose primary industry is tourism, we get a little possessive of our turf. Roma's is ours.

"Sometimes I feel like nothing here ever changes," I say. "If you told me we had to go to class in the morning, I might actually believe you."

Ryan grins. "Except if we had class in the morning, I don't think you'd be here with me."

"Well, it's not like you ever asked me."

"And risk the wrath of Jason and his buddies? No thanks."

"He wasn't that bad."

Ryan raises his eyebrows.

"Okay, he probably was."

"I'm sorry. I probably shouldn't bring him up."

"No, it's actually okay."

"I'll be honest, I'd like to throat punch that guy right about now."

I laugh. Man, it feels good to laugh. "I'd pay good money to see that."

A waitress brings our dinner. Roma's pizza is simple, and greasy, but delicious. Huge slices of pepperoni cover the thick cheese. It's positively sinful.

We chat about the festival a little, but it isn't long before we're on to other things: movies we've seen and want to see, places we've been, where we'd love to go if we had the chance. For me, it's Europe. For Ryan, the Caribbean. Watching him smile, I think I might trade in backpacking through Europe for a white, sandy beach with a shirtless Ryan. We joke and laugh, poking fun at each other. I can't remember the last time I was so relaxed. So free.

I giggle as a string of cheese sticks to my chin. Ryan reaches across the table and runs a finger down my jaw to wipe it off. He sits back with this pensive look on his face, that insanely cute little furrow between his eyes.

"What?"

"Nothing. I just, kind of wondered if I should do this or not. But I'm glad I did."

"Why?"

"Why am I glad? Well, the sight of you with cheese on your face was worth the cost of dinner."

I laugh, but wipe my chin with a napkin, just to be sure. "No, why did you wonder if you should do this?"

He opens his mouth as if he's going to speak, then closes

it again, glancing away. I hesitate, wondering if I shouldn't have asked. I meant it to be flirtatious, a reason for him to say something nice about wanting to see me. Then I could say something sweet back. Isn't that how it works?

I'm so bad at this.

His eyes move back to mine and his dimples pucker with his smile. "I just wasn't sure if you'd want to hang out, you know, outside of official festival business."

My shoulders relax and I smile back. "Yeah, this has been great."

He doesn't reply—just sits there staring at me, his gaze so intense I can't move. What is going on in that head of his? Has this turned into a date yet? Is that what I want? The longer he holds my eyes, the harder my heart pounds in my chest, and the more I think maybe the best thing would be for us to get out of here and go back to his place. Now.

Ryan blinks. "I, um, I need to use the bathroom. I'll be right back."

He leaves to use the restroom and I check my phone, more to anchor myself to some sort of reality than because I want to check my messages. I stare at the screen, not really seeing it. My feelings are a tangled mess, like splashes of color, all mingling and blending together. What is happening to me?

My ears perk up to the conversation in the booth behind me. I swear I heard my name. I don't really want to eavesdrop, but the feeling that they're talking about me is so strong, I lean my head back and listen.

"That's what I heard."

"Wow. I didn't see that coming."

"I know, isn't it strange? I guess she moved back in with her parents."

Oh my god, they are *talking about me.*

"So she left him?"

"I think. Or maybe he kicked her out, I don't know. I heard she's hanging around with that guy who bought the old church up the highway. I can't remember his name. Doesn't that seem kind of fast to you?"

"Totally. It's sad. Some women just can't be alone."

I feel the color drain from my face and my stomach turns over. Is that what people are saying about me? That I can't be alone? I want to turn around and argue—tell them I am a strong, independent, successful woman. I work for a prestigious firm in Seattle and I make my own way in the world. I don't need anyone. But I'm too stunned to do anything other than stare at the table.

Ryan slips back into his seat across from me. "Hey, sorry. Do you want to go get some dessert and a drink somewhere?"

I blink at him. "Um, no. I think I should get home."

"Is everything all right?"

"Yeah," I say, with a flippant wave of my hand. "Everything's fine. I'm just ... not really up for a late night."

My fight or flight urge is taking over and I want to dash outside, away from the prying eyes of the other Roma's patrons. What was I thinking? I just got out of a relationship that lasted my entire adult life up to this point. I can't be running into the arms of another man right now. I don't want people to see me as *that* girl—the one who can't make it on her own. The one who needs a man to be sure of herself.

"Okay," he says, his brow furrowed. "Do you want me to take you home, then?"

No, I don't need you to do anything for me. "That's all right, I'll get home on my own." I gather up my purse and stand, feeling panic rise. I never should have come running home to this town. I'm nothing but a disgrace, and the whole town knows it.

Ryan follows me outside silently. I fire off a quick text to Melissa as I walk.

Please come get me at Roma's. Now. Emergency.

"I'm not sure what just happened, but I can drive you home. It's no big deal."

"No, I'm good. Thanks for dinner, it was nice. I'm sure we'll talk soon. The festival and all."

He looks at me like I'm crazy. Maybe I am. "Do you have a ride coming or something?"

I shrug, trying to act casual and hide my trembling hands. "Melissa's on her way. I, um, I wanted to see her anyway, so it worked out."

"I'll wait, then."

"No, no, it's fine. You don't have to stay."

Ryan takes a few steps back and crosses his arms, but he doesn't head for his car. I watch the road, willing Melissa to get here, tapping my finger against my phone. I don't want those women in the restaurant to come out and see me standing here.

"Nicole, did something happen? Did I say something?"

"No, it's not you. This is just a weird time for me. I need to get home."

"I can—"

Melissa pulls up in front of us like a bat out of hell, her tires squealing. Her car door flies open and she jumps out, her face full of concern. She looks at me, then at Ryan, and her brow furrows.

"Are you all right?" she asks me, giving Ryan a sidelong glance.

Ryan looks bewildered, but I try to ignore him, and the

feeling of guilt that is blooming in my belly. "I'm fine. Let's just go."

"Okay..." Melissa says.

"Thanks again for dinner," I say without looking at Ryan, as I get in Melissa's car.

Melissa shuts her door and pulls out toward the road. "Holy shit, Nic. What the hell did he do?"

Tears flood my eyes. What is wrong with me?

"Nothing. He didn't do anything."

"Then why did I just rescue you from Roma's?"

"I am such a disaster of a person. I had everything. A good-looking boyfriend. A great apartment in an awesome neighborhood. A great job."

"I'm sorry, honey, but I'm totally not following you."

I shake my head and wipe beneath my eyes. "I was voted 'Most Likely to Succeed' in high school, you remember that? Such bullshit. It should have been 'Most Likely to Desperately Need a Man in Her Life.'"

"What the hell are you talking about?"

"Things fall apart with Jason, and what do I do? I come running home to mommy and daddy and cling on to the first guy who's nice to me. What is that about?"

"Wow. Okay, overreact much?"

"I'm not overreacting."

"Sure you aren't," she says, her voice full of sarcasm.

"How did you get there so fast?"

"I was driving home from picking up some stuff at the store." She gestures to a few grocery bags in the back seat.

"Oh, sorry."

"It's fine. I was done, and nothing in there's frozen or anything."

She takes a right where she should go left.

"Where are we going?"

She ignores me. Two turns later, she drives down the beach approach, her headlights hitting the crashing waves. She pulls over to the side at the end of the approach and turns off the car.

"What are you doing?" I ask.

"Giving you a minute to calm the fuck down."

"Do you talk to your students with that mouth?"

"In my head, I do."

Despite myself, I laugh. "Seriously, why are we sitting on the beach?"

"Come on, Nicole. We always used to come down here when we were pissed about something. Our parents, or our dickhead boyfriends. You sat out here with me in your prom dress, missing half the dance, because I was crying over Aaron Sanders dumping me right before the dance."

"That was awful. Showing up at prom with that hussy from another school. I can't even remember her name, that's how forgettable she was."

Melissa laughs so hard she snorts. "Hussy. That's such a fantastic word."

She pauses, taking a deep breath. We both stare out at the water for a few minutes, letting the conversation die. The headlights illuminate the white caps as they crash onto the sand, the rhythm carrying through the closed doors.

"Okay, Nic," she says after a while. "Spill."

"I freaked out. Ryan asked me to dinner and we were having a great time. He's so easy to talk to. I can't remember the last time I felt so comfortable. Even after all those years, I felt like I had to walk on eggshells with Jason. Tonight was so different. I forgot what it was like to just chill and be *me* with someone."

"There's a pretty big disconnect here. How do you go

from that, which sounds lovely, to flipping your shit and calling me in for a dramatic rescue?"

I press my fingers over my eyes. I am such an idiot. "I heard some people at another table talking about me."

"You realize you were probably imagining it."

"No, I wasn't. I heard what they were saying. They called me sad because I'm one of *those* girls who can't be alone."

"Is that what this is about?" She turns in her seat so she's facing me. "First of all, fuck them. They don't know you. They don't know anything that's going on in your life. It's easy to sit around and gossip over a fucking pizza. It's none of their goddamn business."

I lean my head against the seat. "I know."

"No, you don't know. You aren't one of *those* girls. You're Nicole Prescott. You're smart and beautiful, and life just took a big fat dump in your lap. You need to quit spending your precious energy giving a shit what everyone else thinks. Do you know what some people said about me when I started my job at the elementary school? That I must not have been able to make it in the outside world. I had to come running back to the beach after college and go work at the same school I went to. You know what? Fuck them right in the ass. I came back here because this is my home. I love this stupid town. I've wanted to teach at that damn school since forever. So I did. And I love my job, even when those little shits piss me off. I don't care what those gossipy bitches think about me, and you shouldn't care either."

I close my eyes. I know Melissa is right. I envy her ability to brush off other people's opinions. She's always been that way. What people think and say about me seems so important in the moment. But why? What do I care?

"Oh my god, I'm such a horrible person. I just walked out

on him. I freaked out and I ran. He probably thinks it's his fault."

"Yeah, he probably does."

I give Melissa a sidelong glance. "Thanks. That's so helpful."

"You should call him."

She's absolutely right. I bring up his number and hit send. It rings once. Twice. I meet Melissa's eyes. She gives me an encouraging, if worried, smile. Third ring. Fourth. I shake my head slowly and his voicemail picks up. I hang up without leaving a message. I'm not sure what to say, and at least he'll see I tried to call.

"He didn't answer."

"Maybe he turned his phone off."

"Yeah, I guess." But I know he's avoiding my call. "I'll try again tomorrow."

"Sure." She starts engine. "I'll get you home. Unless you want to go get a drink or something."

"Thanks Mel, but no. I think I want to eat a tub of ice cream, then go to bed and berate myself for being an idiot until I fall asleep."

"Sounds productive."

I sigh. I don't know why I have such a hang-up about what people say about me. Melissa is right; it shouldn't matter. Saying I can't help it is a cop out, but that's honestly how it feels. I don't know what it would be like to throw caution to the wind and live my life without looking over my shoulder, without wondering who's judging me.

Maybe I'll go up to Ryan's place in the morning. I owe him at least an in-person apology. I hope he'll be willing to talk to me, but I can't blame him if he isn't.

11

RYAN

My phone lights up with Nicole's number, but I toss it onto the passenger seat without answering. I don't know what just happened, but I don't want to deal with her drama right now. Did someone come in and switch women while I was in the bathroom?

I was in the middle of a fucking fantastic date—and it most certainly turned into a date—when she literally did a one-eighty on me. Damn my bladder. I'd been holding it for a while at that point, but if I knew she'd be all weird when I got back from the bathroom, I would have waited. Did I say something that freaked her out? Did she get a phone call while I was gone?

Oh, shit. I bet she got a call from douchebag Jason.

That makes a little more sense, but it doesn't make me feel any better. My head is spinning. She was so easy to talk to. I can't remember feeling so relaxed with a woman, maybe ever. I dated too many models who sat with me and picked at their food. It was so distracting, watching a woman shift the contents of her plate around, taking tiny bites, clearly calculating the calorie count of each morsel. One woman even brought a protein shake to dinner. She didn't want anything but water for her little shaker bottle—she emptied in that powdered shit, shook it up, and that was that. She spent the rest of the meal watching me eat.

But Nicole—she attacked that pizza with gusto, clearly enjoying her dinner. We laughed and joked around. I found myself telling her stories about my time in L.A. that I never share with anyone.

And when I touched her. Oh my god. What was that? I wanted to grab her by the wrist and pull her out to my car, and who knew if we'd make it anywhere? I wanted to know what she tasted like, what her hot ass would feel like in my hands. My constant hard-on throughout dinner aside, I thought we were having fun. It was so easy with her.

Until it wasn't.

What did Jason want? I know some girls have a hard time leaving a guy, even if they've been hurt. And she was with him a long time. Maybe he had something she couldn't resist. I have no idea what that would be, but I never understood why she was with him in the first place. And if it wasn't Jason, then what had happened?

I step on the gas, flying up the highway. With the way this night is going, I'll probably get a ticket, but I don't care. I just want to get away from town, back to the solitude of my place. I have a shoot in the morning, so I need time to relax so I can be on my game. I pride myself on giving my clients my best, no matter what I'm shooting.

Tomorrow I have a boudoir session, and those are so intimate. I love doing them. Women absolutely fascinate me —their curves, their strength, their fragility, their sensuality. Bringing that out in a photograph feels like magic, especially when my subject isn't a paid model. Regular, everyday women, with their folds and wrinkles and curves in the wrong places. They all have this fire, this passion inside of them. A beauty that goes beyond the shape of their bodies. It's exciting to bring that out.

Truth be told, it's a fucking turn-on, even if I'm not attracted to the woman I'm shooting. There's this moment, when they finally let their inhibitions drop—when they relax and let out the inner sexuality they've been repressing. God, it's glorious.

But if I'm going to bring that out in my client in the morning, I need to get Nicole out of my mind.

I spend the night tossing and turning. My bed is usually my favorite thing. It's so damn comfortable, I always fall asleep seconds after my head hits the pillow. But I can't sleep. The bed feels too big. Too empty.

This is stupid. Whatever spooked Nicole, she obviously has issues she needs to work through. Whether it's douchebag Jason, or something else, it's not up to me to fix her. I can barely hold myself together.

Morning comes too soon, and I make a big pot of coffee. I wander out into my studio to set things up for my shoot. My client, Joanna, is someone I tried to work with before, but she got too anxious and decided to reschedule. She's a sweet lady, in her forties with a couple kids. She isn't a local, but she's staying at a hotel in Jetty Beach, with friends if I recall. Making a girl's weekend out of her boudoir session. Hopefully her girlfriends have given her some courage so she'll be able to relax and get through her shoot this time. The first time we met, she told me all about her husband and her marriage. They usually do. Sometimes it feels like I'm part therapist. Like a lot of the women I work with, she loves her husband, but life in the bedroom is pretty quiet. She hopes to rekindle the fire with some sexy photos.

I can definitely help with that.

I move a few things around, wanting to create the perfect setting. Joanna will be nervous, so she needs to feel at ease, and the props I choose will either help or hinder. I don't think she's going to be a lingerie or corset kind of woman. I encourage women to bring their own clothes, but I also have a pretty wide assortment of pieces in a variety of sizes. I often ask to keep samples when I do shoots for product lines, and the companies are generally willing to let me have them. I pull out a couple of evening gowns and a few silky slips, and hang them on a freestanding metal rack. I'll start with those and see what she gravitates toward. From there, I can help her find some pieces that make her feel good. Because that's what this is all about. Making her feel good. It doesn't matter if the color flatters her skin or the cut is just right. If she feels sexy, her photos will radiate sex appeal.

I move the chaise out of the way. I don't see Joanna on burgundy velvet. Too brazen. She needs soft. Calm. I move a few racks with billowing white curtains for the backdrop and angle the white couch in front of them. Maybe I'll start with her there. If I can get her comfortable, I bet she'll feel sexy as hell holding up a sheet, turning to look at the camera. I'll tousle her hair, add a little flush to her cheeks. Give her that post-sex glow. I smile thinking about it. She's going to feel amazing.

I take a quick shower and throw on some clean clothes —a pair of slacks and a light blue button-down shirt. I cuff the sleeves, rolling them up so I have ease of movement, and get to work setting up my lights and equipment.

Someone knocks on the front door and I look at the clock. Joanna is early, but I'm almost ready for her. I give the studio one last glance, hoping she'll like what she sees. She's come all this way for the second time—I really want to make her comfortable and have a fantastic shoot.

I open the door and nervousness shoots through my gut. It's Nicole.

She looks incredible. Her blond hair is pulled back with a little braid on each side, a few pieces hanging down around her ivory neck. The dark blue of her dress makes her eyes glow, and her white sweater ends just above her waistline, showing off the curve of her hips. Her lips glisten and I can't stop staring as she opens and closes her mouth a few times.

"Hi," I say finally, willing myself not to ogle her chest. The neckline of her dress dips just enough...

"Hey," she says and my eyes snap to hers. "I, um.... This is embarrassing. Can I come in?"

She kind of shunned me the night before, but I find myself stepping aside and ushering her in. I close the door and hesitate there, catching a whiff of her scent when she walks by. It's lightly floral, soft and sweet. I swallow hard.

"Listen, I came here to apologize. Last night ... I don't even know what to say. I was having a really nice time, but I kind of freaked out. It was a stupid thing to do, and it wasn't your fault at all. I realized after I left what a jerk I was being, and I feel so bad."

I'm not sure what to say. It was so strange. I rub the back of my neck. "It's okay. I guess you caught me off guard. I wasn't sure what happened."

"I know.". She sounds so miserable. I want to scoop her up in my arms and make her feel better. "I'm sorry I came unannounced, but I wasn't sure if you'd take my call. I was up half the night feeling terrible for how I treated you."

My cock strains against my pants, as if I can set it free and it will attack her of its own free will. My fingertips tingle with the desire to touch her. I open my mouth to say she isn't a jerk, when another knock at the door almost makes me jump.

"I actually have a client this morning."

"Oh, no." Her eyebrows draw down and her shoulders slump. "I'm so sorry. I'll go."

I kind of don't want her to go, but it isn't like I can let her stay while I shoot Joanna. And why do I want her to stay? My urge to make her feel better is so strong. I want to reach out and draw her close, kiss away the furrows in that adorable brow, work my way down. I move to open the door, trying to get that image out of my mind.

Joanna's anxious face greets me. She's done her makeup, and her light brown hair hangs loose. She has a handbag over one shoulder and a duffel bag in her hands.

I take a deep breath. "Hey, Joanna. It's good to see you. Come on in."

"Hi, Ryan," she says, her voice a bit shaky. She comes in and sets down her bag, then smiles at Nicole.

"Hi, sorry," Nicole says. "I'm Nicole."

"I'm so relieved," Joanna says. "I love that you have a female assistant this time. I think that will help a lot. I'm so sorry about our last session."

Female assistant? Oh, shit. "No, don't worry about it at all. I want you to be relaxed. Think of our last appointment as a getting-to-know-you session. I learned more about you, and you had a chance to get comfortable with me."

"That's true," she says. "I still haven't told my husband about any of this. That's why I came out here with friends this time. I didn't want him to get the wrong idea and think I was coming to the beach for some other reason."

"No, we don't want that." I flash her a warm smile. "Why don't you go take a look at the setting I've put together for you, and see if any of the clothing on the rack over there is to your liking. You can wear something of your own, or I brought out a few selections for you to try. Find something that makes you feel good. There's a screen over there, you can step behind it and change."

Joanna nods with a smile. She already seems more relaxed than she was last time. Nicole stands in one spot, a classic deer-in-headlights look on her face. I wait until Joanna is busy looking at the clothes, and move closer to Nicole.

"Listen, Joanna is a really sweet client. This is her second try for a boudoir session—last time she was too anxious and we never took any pictures. If having you here makes her comfortable..." I trail off, hoping Nicole will be willing to stay. It's sweet that she came to apologize and the truth is, I don't want her to leave, not until we have more of a chance to talk. If she can help me with my client, that's even better.

"I have no idea what I'm doing. I'm afraid I'll get in your way."

I shake my head. "You won't. I'll tell you what to do." She draws in a quick breath and her cheeks turn the slightest shade of pink. *Fuck, that was hot. Please don't look at my pants. I can't handle your eyes on my cock right now.* "Maybe you could go make Joanna a mimosa? I have the stuff in my fridge."

"Yes." Her expression relaxes. "I can do that."

I try to discreetly adjust my pants as I walk over to Joanna. The last thing I need to do is freak her out with my bulging dick. I smile at her, telling myself to keep it professional. Nicole doesn't need to be a distraction. She'll help Joanna feel good about her session.

Yep. I can do this.

12

NICOLE

My heart flutters while I pop the cork on the bottle of champagne in Ryan's kitchen. I spent the entire drive to his house petrified, sure he would either ignore me or shut the door in my face. I thought my apology was going okay, but then his client arrived. That was a curve ball I didn't see coming. My first thought when he answered the door was how much I wanted to stay. Everything feels so unfinished between us. I don't want to leave without knowing whether or not he forgives me.

And the way he looks, dressed all nice for his client. I'm so lame, I practically fanned myself. The sleeves of his button-down shirt strain against his muscular arms and his hands look strong, yet dexterous. Of course I checked out his ass when he answered the door. I did not know a man could make simple slacks look that good. I want to take a bite out of it.

I pour the champagne into a fluted glass, leaving room for a splash of orange juice, and let out a deep breath. *Get yourself together, Nicole. You need to be professional.* I'm nervous about helping on his shoot—I wasn't kidding when

I said I have no idea what I'm doing. Ryan said he'd tell me what to do. Why did those words make my panties wet?

I add a splash of orange juice and put the glass on a little silver tray he has sitting on the counter. There's a bowl of washed strawberries next to the sink, so I cut the stems off a few, add them to a little plate, and put everything on the tray. Champagne and strawberries are such a decadent touch. I notice he has a box of fancy chocolates sitting out as well. Wow, this guy thinks of everything.

Ryan is adjusting the lights in the studio when I come out. He moves one, then steps back, tilting his head to the side to study the composition. Soft music plays in the background—something classical, and just loud enough to give the room a soothing ambiance. Joanna is behind a large folding screen, so I wait nearby, holding the tray like a waitress. She emerges in a flowing beige gown with a deep neckline. It looks fabulous on her, but I can tell by her body language that she's unsure of herself.

"Here." I hold out the tray. She gives me a grateful smile and takes the champagne flute.

"Thanks," she says. "I think I'll need this."

"You don't have anything to be nervous about." My eyes flick to Ryan. "You're in great hands."

He gives me his lopsided grin and a tingle runs down my spine.

"Okay, Joanna, take your time," Ryan says. "When you're ready, we'll do a few test shots. There's no pressure, I'm just going to be sure of the lighting."

Joanna takes a quick breath and hands me her half-empty glass. Ryan positions her on the white couch, laying her across it horizontally, her back propped up with pillows. She fusses with her dress while Ryan gets his camera.

"Just sit back and relax," he says. "I'll even delete these.

Don't worry about posing or smiling or anything."

He takes a few shots, bringing his camera down to look at the screen in between. He adjusts a few lights and takes another. Joanna lays on the couch, looking a bit stiff, and plucks at the gown.

"All right," he says. "This looks really good. Now, we'll start slow. I don't want you to worry about anything. Take a few deep breaths, maybe another sip of champagne."

I dart in and give her the drink. She takes a long swallow and sets it back on the tray.

"Perfect. You look lovely." Ryan's voice has gone soft and low, sending shivers through me. "This is going to sound strange, but clench your hands into fists for a second. Good. Now let them go, relax your fingers. Perfect. Do the same with your shoulders. Scrunch them up, hold there. Now release."

Ryan walks around a light and regards her with that head tilt again. He hasn't taken any pictures other than the first shots to test his lighting. "Next, close your eyes. Just soft, don't squeeze them shut. Now, I'm going to come near you and you're going to feel me touch your hair a little." Joanna's eyes drift closed and Ryan moves in. He adjusts her hair, running his fingers through it and teasing it out, messing it up a little. He lifts her chin with a finger and smooths the folds of her dress.

"You're doing beautifully, Joanna," he says. "Don't do it yet, but when I give you the word, you're going to open your eyes. Slowly. You're relaxed and happy. Satisfied. Your body feels warm. The couch is soft beneath you, your dress whispers across your skin. Open."

Joanna's eyes flutter open and her lips part. Ryan snaps a few pictures.

"Beautiful," Ryan says, absolute sincerity in his tone. "Let your head move to the right ever so slightly. Good. Now, stay relaxed. Trust me. These look incredible already, but I think we can do better. Go deeper."

Deeper sends a jolt through me.

"All right," Joanna says.

"Move your hips just a little," Ryan says.

"Ryan, I don't know—"

"Shh," he says, putting a finger to his lips. "No talking for a few minutes. In fact, you're not allowed to talk right now."

Oh, damn.

Joanna squeaks out a short reply but Ryan smiles at her, dimples and all, and she goes silent. I stand, transfixed, and almost drop the tray. It bobbles in my hand, but I recover before anything falls. Instead of inviting disaster, I set it down on a side table.

"Move your hips, Joanna. Rock them back and forth a tiny bit. Don't be afraid. You can trust me. Now open your knees a bit. Not too much yet. Good. Take your hands and run them up and down your thighs. Lightly, just to relax your legs. Good. Now let your left leg drop open. Yes, your foot can dangle down to the floor, that's perfect."

He talks to her in his velvety voice, easing her into slight variations of her position. Her eyes follow him as he moves around her. He takes pictures from different angles, consulting the screen on the back of his camera in between shots. His steady stream of encouragement and commands goes on.

Dropping to one knee, he shoots another picture. "This is amazing, Joanna. Let's do something else. What does your husband like? What part of you is his favorite?"

"Oh gosh, I don't know," she says.

"Come on, Joanna," Ryan says, coaxing her. "Breasts, backside?"

"I can't believe I'm doing this," she says. "Um, backside, I guess."

"Sit up and we're going to have you get on your knees with your hands on the back of the couch. Perfect."

He grabs a white sheet from a nearby table and hands it to me. I take it and he leans in close, speaking low into my ear. "I want to get her undressed for this next bit, but I think she'll do it for you rather than me. I want the sheet draped around her, and she can hold the front up over her chest. I'll come in and adjust it."

I nod and gently shake the sheet open.

"Okay, Joanna, you're doing amazing. Stay with me. Nicole's going to come over with a sheet. She'll help you slip off the gown and you can hold the sheet around yourself."

"I—"

"I said no talking, remember?"

I dart in and put the sheet on the couch, then lift her gown over her head. She lets me undress her without a hint of protest. She's wearing a lacy thong and pretty matching bra. I glance back at Ryan.

He mouths, *Bra off*.

I try to mimic Ryan's soothing tone. "Okay, Joanna, I'm going to unhook your bra, but you can hold this sheet up."

She holds still while I take off her bra, slipping the straps off her shoulders. I drape the sheet over her, giving her the edge to hold up over her breasts. Her breath comes fast but she complies, and I adjust the sheet around her, leaving it to cascade down the side of her leg. Her backside is bare, save for the strip of thong; the lighting glints off her skin.

I move out of the way and Ryan takes a couple shots without saying anything. Joanna holds still, her posture rigid.

"Look at me," Ryan says, a sharp note of command in his voice. My eyes immediately dart to him. Joanna turns her neck and he snaps a few more pictures.

"Imagine a hand sliding up your back." Ryan moves while he talks, finding a new angle. "It's strong and warm. It runs up to your neck, fingers brushing through your hair." Joanna's head drifts back. "The hand runs down, caressing your silky soft skin. The fingers trail down your backside and slip between your thighs."

I swallow hard, heat building between my legs. Joanna sucks in a breath and arches her back. Something in her posture changes. Her shoulders relax and her ass tilts back, giving her a sensual silhouette.

Ryan has a look of triumph on his face. "Take your hand and run it up and down your body. Perfect. Lean your head back and let your hair cascade down your back. Two hands are on you now. They grip your hips. You want this. You want him to come in behind you and press himself against you. Look at me. Fingers tease between your thighs, running between the soft folds. Gentle pressure in just the right spot. It sends a thrill through you, a burst of pleasure."

Oh my god.

He moves in again and adjusts the sheet, then backs away a few steps. He talks faster. "Run your hand down your stomach. Stop. Look at me. You do what I say, you hear me, Joanna?"

She gives a feeble nod.

"Let the sheet drop and hold your breasts. They feel good in your hands. His hands are on you too, touching, caressing. Your skin tingles everywhere. He slips his fingers inside you. He knows how to touch you, moving in and out, circling, curling. He rubs his thumb on your clit and you can barely stand it. You want more. You want him inside you."

My heart races and my skin is on fire.

"This is amazing, Joanna," he says. "Look at me over your other shoulder. You're beautiful like this."

She is. The anxious woman is gone and in her place is a gorgeous, sexual being. She doesn't have a model's body, but Ryan seems to know how to get her to move to accent every curve and show her from the best angle. Her body is relaxed, yet alive. Ryan continues shooting, moving in to adjust a detail, then moving out again to take more photos.

He stands and looks down at his camera again. "These are incredible. I think we have everything we need."

Joanna seems to melt. She looks around for the sheet, as if she suddenly realizes she's almost naked. I rush in and help her pull the sheet around her.

She blinks, as if coming out of a trance. Her lips turn up in a slow smile. "I did it?"

Ryan comes closer. "You were unbelievable."

He catches my eye and holds my gaze. My panties are drenched, my pussy so hot I can hardly stand it. The memory of his words washes over me.

Joanna stands, holding the sheet around herself. "I'm sorry, I don't know what came over me."

"There's no need to apologize," Ryan says. "This was absolutely perfect."

She goes back behind the screen to change. I keep my eyes on the ground. I don't dare look up at Ryan. The back of my neck burns with his gaze, but I know if I meet his eyes, I won't be able to control myself. I've never felt anything like this in my entire life—this burning need. It consumes me.

"Wait here," Ryan says, in that same soft, soothing voice he's been using. I don't dream of disobeying him. His voice is my world, my reality. I wait, breathing hard.

13

RYAN

It takes every ounce of self-control I have to finish up with Joanna. I wait for her to dress, give her a bottled water, and explain when she can expect to hear from me regarding the finished photos. My dick feels like it's going to burst. Concentration is almost impossible, and I stumble over my words more than once. Nicole's presence in my studio calls to me like a siren's song. I'm entranced.

I've never taken my coaxing quite that far with a client before. Every word was what I want to do to Nicole. Still, I made myself hold back, images flashing through my mind that I didn't dare give voice to. It worked better than I could have imagined. Joanna was as pliable as soft clay, doing everything I asked of her. She dropped her inhibitions and showed me the side of herself I knew was there. And I captured it all.

But all I can think about is Nicole.

Nicole doesn't move while I usher Joanna outside, her eyes locked on the floor in front of her. Did I scare her? Repulse her? Not everyone will understand what I do. They'll see it as inappropriate, or like I'm taking advantage of my clients. All I want is to bring out their inner passion. To stoke the flame that every woman carries, and help them remember they are desirable.

"Nicole."

I let her name hang in the air. Nicole breaths hard. Her scent tickles my nose and I move closer, afraid I might scare her away.

"Look at me."

She turns her head toward me, her eyes blinking slowly, her lips open. Her face is deliciously flushed. I want her so bad it sends shockwaves through my limbs. My cock throbs. I take a few more steps, holding her eyes with mine.

Nicole's tongue darts out to lick her lips. *Fuck me. Should I do it? Should I pounce before she gets away?* I stalk her, moving like a cat on the hunt, easing my way closer.

I stop mere inches away. My breath comes fast, and my eyes devour her. She's so close, I can feel her body heat, tempting me. She's tantalizing. Her collarbone stands out with each breath, her breasts straining against her dress. *I should go slowly. Soft and sweet for Nicole.* I hesitate, holding myself in check, stretching out the agony.

Until she bites her lower lip. Then I'm done for.

I surge in, grabbing the back of her neck, and pull her mouth to mine. Her body melts against me, her hands slipping around my waist. I suck her lower lip into my mouth and let my bottom teeth drag across it—not so hard that it hurts, but enough that she gasps. I moan as she presses into me, rubbing her body against my swollen cock, and let her lip go.

"Ryan."

She says my name and grabs my cock through my pants. Why are we wearing these fucking clothes?

"Oh my god, Nicole, I need you. I fucking need to be inside you right now."

Breathlessly, she nods. I yank her sweater off and let it fall to the floor. We back up toward the couch, pulling our clothes off like they're on fire. I grab her, pulling her close, and rub my hands down her back. Her breasts press into me and her skin against mine is amazing. I bury my face in her neck, her scent filling me. Grabbing her ass, I squeeze, pushing my cock against her.

Nicole groans. "I want you inside me, Ryan. I want it now."

Her voice centers me. I could throw her down on the couch and pound her until I come. But this is Nicole Prescott. I never dreamed I'd have her naked in my studio, begging me to fuck her. This is not something I can rush.

I push the pillows aside and lay her down on the couch. Instead of climbing on top of her, I get on my knees and push her legs apart. She's almost bare, just a sexy as hell triangle left in front. Fuck me, that's hot. I slide my hands down her thighs and she tilts her hips up.

"Don't make me wait," she says.

I lean in and trail my hand down, feeling the soft folds of skin. "You're already so wet." I tease my fingers up and down, exploring. She shivers and moans, but when her fingers dig into the cushions and her back arches, I know I found the right spot. I push two fingers inside her and massage her clit with my thumb.

"Oh god, Ryan."

I circle my thumb around her clit, varying the pressure, learning. "Does this feel good?"

"I love it."

"This?" I press harder.

Her mouth opens and she moans again. I love that

sound. It makes me want to drive her crazy so she won't stop. I lean down and kiss the inside of her thigh, move across to kiss the other. I work my way up, trailing my tongue up her legs, until I reach her center.

Nicole shudders as I run my tongue up and down her slit. She's swollen, so sensitive she reacts to every tiny movement. I find her clit with my mouth, and she gasps.

"You taste so good. I could do this to you forever."

"Holy shit, Ryan," she says, breathless. "I've never."

I pause. Does she mean...? "Has no one ever done this for you?"

"No."

You have got to be fucking kidding me. Douchebag Jason had her all those years, and he never tasted her? What the fuck is wrong with that guy?

A smile creeps over my face. "Oh, Nicole. I have a treat for you."

Sweeping my tongue up and down, I rub her clit with quick strokes. She tastes so good. I grab her ass and she lets her legs rest over my shoulders. I bury my face in her, pushing my tongue into her pussy, dragging it out again and again. Her body is stiff at first, like she's afraid. Holding back.

"I'm going to make you come like this."

"I don't know if I can."

I lift my head just enough to meet her eyes. "Look at me."

She meets my gaze, her eyes tight with anxiety.

"Watch."

I run my tongue over her clit. Her mouth drops open and her eyes roll back.

"You're going to come for me."

I go to work on her, rubbing my tongue up and down. I feel for her responses, trying different speeds and pressures.

When her hips begin to move with my rhythm, I know I have her.

Her legs open wider and I suck her clit into my mouth. Goddamn, this is so fucking hot. I have my mouth all over Nicole Prescott's pussy, and her body is writhing beneath me.

"What are you doing to me?"

I push my fingers inside and press my tongue against her. Up and down, in and out. I try a little softer, then a little harder, feeling her body react. She groans, her hips rocking up and down. I keep going, moaning into her. She cries out. She seems to like more pressure, so I concentrate just above her opening, letting my fingers push in and out, my tongue massaging her.

"Oh, Ryan."

She's so hot. I want my cock inside her—to feel that slick pussy all over me. But she needs to come for me first. I'm not going to stop until she does.

I hold to a rhythm that has her thrusting her hips into me. Faster. Harder. Her pussy clenches around my fingers, her folds burning hot under my tongue.

"Oh my god."

I keep rubbing my tongue up and down as her orgasm builds, moving with her grinding hips. She calls out with each pulse, her entire body shuddering with pleasure.

When she finishes, I make my way back down her thighs, kissing her as I go, tasting her sweet skin. Her chest rises and falls, her nipples pink, a light sheen of sweat on her forehead.

"How was it?" I grin at her.

She blinks as if she's dazed, shaking her head slowly. "I don't even... I can't..."

I run my hands up and down her legs and scoot closer,

letting my swollen cock rub against her thigh. Her pussy is there, dripping wet, waiting for me. I don't know how this is happening, or whether I'll ever have this chance again. Have I ever been this turned on in my entire life? I grab her hips and squeeze, pressing myself close.

"What do you want, Nicole?"

"I want you inside me."

My heart hammers and my dick throbs. A little voice shouts at me from the back of my mind. "Shit, Nicole, I don't have anything."

She blinks at me. "No, it's okay. I'm still on the pill."

A wicked smile steals across my face. "Where do you want it?"

"Inside me," she says. "Please."

Fuck, that little voice begging me. It's almost too much. She's so delicious, quivering beneath me. Her hair already a mess. Her cheeks flushed. Her nipples hard. I lean over her, grabbing her ass with one hand, and take her breast in my mouth. I let my cock rub against her wet folds, teasing her, and flick my tongue over her nipple.

I look up and she's panting.

"What do you want?"

She lifts her head and meets my eyes. "I want you to fuck me."

14

NICOLE

He plunges into me. I've never felt anything like it. He fills me up, stretching me, the slightest tinge of pain enhancing the unbelievable pleasure.

I just had an orgasm. How am I ready for more? He moves in and out, hitting me with just the right amount of pressure with each thrust. I open my legs wider and grab his ass, pushing him in deeper.

"I love the way you fill me. You fill every bit of me. I had no idea."

He pushes in and pulls out. I want him to move faster, but he holds back.

"Careful, baby. This is too good."

I hold his ass tighter, digging in my fingers. I rock my hips, dragging his cock across my clit with each thrust. The pressure builds in waves. I want more. I want all of him.

"Oh my god, Nicole. You're amazing."

My name on his lips is sublime. He leans down and kisses me, plundering my mouth with his tongue. For half a second, I'm afraid. His mouth has just been ... but it tastes incredible. My flavor mixes with his, and it sends me into a tailspin.

He moves down my neck, sliding his tongue across my skin. I can't believe he's lasted this long.

"Ryan, you feel so good."

He thrusts in and stops, holding tight against me. Jolts of pleasure spread as he grinds his cock in harder.

"What do you want?"

I don't know what to say. I've never been asked that before.

"Tell me. You have to tell me or I won't play." He slides his cock out halfway and pauses, looking at me with a grin that is downright mischievous.

"I don't know."

"If Nicole doesn't know what she wants..." He pulls out a little more.

"No, please. I'll beg. Don't stop."

"Then tell me."

"Push it in, hard."

He does.

I groan, but he doesn't move again.

"Again. Out, but not all the way. Stop there. Push it in. Oh my god. Yes, right there. Pull out again." I grab his ass again and guide him, moving his cock in and out of me.

"What else do you want?"

"Your mouth on my breasts." What am I saying? But I do want it. "Suck on my nipple. Oh my god, yes." I shudder.

"I love it when you tell me what you like."

He holds himself up with one hand and grabs my ass with the other. His muscles flex and ripple. His tattoo covers one shoulder, and he has another on his chest. He's gorgeous. His green eyes rove over my face and the stubble on his jaw is hot as hell. It felt unreal against my thighs and between my legs.

"Faster," I say.

He picks up the pace, pounding his cock into me. Pressure builds again, from deep inside. What is that?

"Don't stop that."

I don't think I'll be able to have another orgasm. On the rare occasions I've climaxed during sex in the past, I was spent afterward, without any desire to continue. But Ryan's tongue was like an appetizer, revving me up for the main course. Pleasure fills me, the intensity increasing.

"Whoa," he says suddenly and slows down. He blows out a breath and holds, the crown of his cock just inside.

I move to push him back in, but he stops me.

"Hang on, baby. I don't want to come too soon."

"Are you almost?"

"Yeah," he says and takes another breath. "Right there. But I want to come together."

He can *do* that?

My body wants more, but I wait. Ryan stares at me. What's going through his head? How did this happen?

He pushes back in and I cry out.

"Yeah, let me hear you. This is incredible, Nicole. Fuck, you feel so good. I could do this all day."

"Oh my god, yes."

Without warning, he pulls out and, like a gymnast, flips us over so he's on the bottom.

"I want to watch you come like this," he says. "You're so beautiful."

I straddle him and lower myself onto his cock. This is delicious. He wants to play with me? Maybe I can play with him.

"Tell me what you want," I say, lifting my ass so his tip is barely touching me.

"Oh no. That's my game."

"Not anymore." I slide down a little, then pull back again. "Tell me."

He puts his hands on my hips and pulls me toward him. "Down. That's it."

"Now what?"

"Move back and forth," he says, guiding me with his hands. "Oh fuck, yes."

I slide up and down, grinding my pussy into him with every stroke.

"Faster."

I pick up the pace, tilting my hips, riding him. His hands move from my hips to my waist and up to my breasts.

"You feel so incredible, Nicole. Do you want to come like this?"

I have choices?

"Yes."

His hands go back to my hips and he moves me faster, pushing me back and forth across his cock. The tip rubs me in just the right spot every time and I feel my inner muscles contracting, the tension mounting. I've never felt anything so deep before.

"Come with me, Nicole," he says. "Fuck me, this is unreal. I want you to come with me."

"Do it."

"Are you sure?"

"Oh my god, do it now. Come in me, Ryan."

The pulses of his cock as he climaxes send me over the edge. An orgasm rocks through me, like nothing I've ever experienced before. My core muscles tense and release, sending explosions of pleasure through my whole body. I throw my head back and ride his wave, letting the mad rush of sensation overtake me.

When I finish, I look down. He smiles, his dimples standing out beneath his stubble.

"Come here." He threads his hand around the back of my neck and draws me down to him. He kisses me, long and slow, his touch so gentle. Our lips part and I draw back. He places a hand across my cheek. "Did that just happen?"

"I think it did."

I get off him and look around. I feel like I forgot where I am. This is Ryan's studio. I just watched him do a photo shoot. And then he fucked me senseless.

Wait, what?

Just when I start to panic, he gets up and puts his arms around me, kissing the top of my head.

"Come in here. I'll help."

Bewildered, I let him lead me through his apartment and into the bathroom. It gleams with newness. Light gray tile contrasts with a dark wood vanity. The fixtures are sleek and modern. A touch of turquoise brakes up the neutrals.

He runs a washcloth under the water and wrings it out. I literally have no idea what he's doing. I thought he'd lead me to the bathroom so I could clean up, but he isn't leaving.

Still naked, he kneels on the mat and runs his hands down my legs. He spreads my thighs apart, his hands strong but gentle, and wipes each inner thigh with the warm washcloth.

Is he kidding right now?

No one, and by no one I mean Jason, has ever done something like this for me. Of course, after what just happened, I realize there are a lot of things Jason never did for me. But this—wiping a soft, wet cloth over my legs with such tenderness. It unmakes me.

Tears spring to my eyes and I cover my mouth. I don't want him to see me cry. I'm standing naked in his bathroom while he washes me—how can I sob in front of him like this?

There's no stopping it. I'm completely overwhelmed and the tears won't stop. My shoulders shake, my hand still clamped to my mouth.

Ryan stands, setting the washcloth on the counter. He touches my face and runs his fingers through my hair. "Nicole, I'm so sorry. Was that too much? I thought we were both ... I thought you wanted that."

I nod through the sobs, trying to speak, but my words are garbled. "I did," I manage finally.

"Come here." He wraps his arm around my shoulders and draws me into his apartment. The king-size bed sprawls across the middle of the space. He eases me into his bed and draws the sheets up over me. "Do you want me to leave you alone?"

There's so much concern in his voice. So much tenderness. My eyes burn with fresh tears.

"No," I whisper. "Please don't go."

He smiles, looking relieved, and climbs into bed with me. He lays on his back and I tuck my head against his shoulder, my arm draped across his chest. My body still tingles with everything he did to me. I take slow, deep breaths, finding calm. For a second, I wonder if I should be embarrassed. I literally had the best sex of my entire life, and it left me a crying mess in his bathroom. Aren't women supposed to cry when sex is *bad*? Certainly not when it's good. But the way Ryan holds me, softly rubbing his fingers across my arm ... I'm not worried. He isn't judging me.

I close my eyes, feeling his warmth envelop me, and drift off to sleep.

15

RYAN

Nicole's body rests against mine, her breathing slow and even. I stare at the ceiling, so relaxed I could fall asleep. I stay awake, a little afraid that if I drift off, I'll wake to find it didn't happen. That was ... fuck me, it was incredible. I'm no stranger to good sex, but Nicole blew me away.

Just like in a good photography session, there was that moment, the instant when her inhibitions fell and her inner goddess broke free. She was hesitant at first—trusting, but hesitant. That willingness to relax with me and let me lead her to a new place was so damn hot. Her taste. Her body. Her skin. Her eyes. Boring into me, wanting me. God, I could do that over and over again. I want to free her. To bring out the passion she's been holding back for so long.

My cock stirs and I take a few deep breaths to calm it down. She's so serene and peaceful. I don't want to disturb her.

I worry a little about her reaction in the bathroom. Elise cried a lot, but ... I don't want to think about Elise. This is about Nicole. I'll talk to her when she wakes up, make sure she's okay. I want to draw her out and give her things she's never experienced, but I don't want to push her too far. Hopefully she was simply taken by surprise.

When she showed up at my door, I had no idea it would end with me taking her on the couch in my studio. A slow grin spreads over my face. I can't help it. I haven't felt this amazing in so long—nope, scratch that. Maybe ever.

For the first time in a very long time, I have a glimmer of hope for my future. Maybe being the reclusive photographer living in an old church on the beach isn't the end of my story.

NICOLE STIRS, rousing me from half-sleep. She makes a cute little noise in her throat, then gasps, lifting her head.

"Hi, beautiful." I brush her hair back from her face and one corner of her mouth turns up in a smile.

"Hey. Sorry. I think I fell asleep."

"That's okay. I'm glad you were so relaxed."

Spots of color rise on her cheeks. She sits up, drawing the sheet over her chest. Her hair falls forward across her face.

I sit up and tuck her hair behind her ear. "Hey. Look at me."

She tilts her chin up to meet my gaze. Her eyes glisten with tears. "I'm sorry. I don't know what's wrong with me."

A single tear breaks free and trails down her cheek. I swipe it away with my thumb.

"There's nothing wrong with you.". My chest tightens with concern. Does she regret this? "Did I do things you didn't like?"

"No," she says, vehemently. "It was incredible. Literally, the best I've ever had. I'm not even exaggerating when I say that."

"Then what's wrong?"

She takes a shaky breath. "I'm overwhelmed, Ryan. I've never... No one has ever... I'm sorry, I'm not making any sense. I feel like I don't know how to do this."

"If you want to tell me something, you can. You can tell me anything."

Her lips fall open, and of course I think about what her mouth would look like around my cock. *Stop it, Ryan. She's having a moment here.*

"There, see, you're doing it again, being all wonderful." She adjusts the sheet, tucking it under her arm. "My only first time with someone was my actual first time, and considering we were dumb teenagers and had no idea what we were doing, I'm sure you can imagine how that went."

"Well, we can't all be born sex gods."

That makes her laugh. "I guess not. It's probably a big no-no to talk about someone else you've slept with when you're still in bed with someone new, but Jason never..." She shakes her head. "He never did anything like what you just did to me. It's not only that you did things I didn't even know were possible. You were so concerned with what I was feeling. I've never had that before. With Jason it was just pump, pump, do your thing, and maybe he'd get me off if I was already in the mood."

Fucking douchebag Jason.

"I'm sorry, I probably freaked you out when I started crying." She swipes her fingers beneath her eyes. "I was just ... overcome."

"Do you feel better now?"

"Yeah. I feel a lot better. I feel great, actually." She looks around the room. "I'm going to sound like an idiot, but I don't know what happens now."

"What do you mean?"

Her cheeks flush. She's adorable.

"I mean, am I supposed to stay? Do I get up and go? I was with one guy for ten years. This is all new to me."

"Do you want to go?" *Say no.*

"No." She bites her lower lip. It's the sweetest little nervous tic.

I run my thumb along her mouth. "Then stay."

"Are you sure?"

"Absolutely. It's Saturday. Do you have to work or anything? What did you have planned?"

She shrugs. "No, I don't have to work. To be honest, this morning I didn't think past what I was going to say to you. I'm really sorry about that, by the way."

"You said that already. I think we're good."

My phone vibrates on the nightstand and I glance at the screen to see who it is. "I'm sorry, it's my mom. She worries if I don't answer."

"No, it's fine."

I pick up the phone and answer. "Hi, Mom."

"Hi, honey. How are you today?"

"I'm, um, I'm really good."

"That's nice to hear," she says. "You sound good. What have you been doing this morning?"

I grin at Nicole. "What have I been doing?" Nicole covers her mouth and giggles. "Well, I had a photo shoot this morning and it went well."

"Oh how lovely. I'm glad you're keeping busy."

"Yes, Mom, I'm keeping busy."

"So everyone's coming to dinner tonight. Can you make it?"

"Tonight? I thought dinner was on Monday."

"It was honey, but I changed it to tonight."

There's something in her tone. "Is everything okay, Mom?"

"Yes, everything's fine. Just be here by six. Don't be late. What do you want for dessert?"

"Whatever you want to make is fine with me."

"I have lemons. Lemon bars?"

"Lemon bars are delicious." I meet Nicole's eyes again and smile, shaking my head. She still has the sheet held up, but one side slips, revealing the curve of her breast. I suddenly very much do *not* want to be talking to my mother. "Listen, Mom, I have a lot of work to do. I'll see you at six, okay?"

"Sounds good, honey. I'll see you then."

I hang up and put down the phone. "Sorry."

"Don't ever apologize for talking to your mother. She seems really sweet."

"She is. She's just ... she worries."

For a second, I think about inviting Nicole to dinner with my parents. I open my mouth, but stop myself. Bringing a woman home to my family is a big deal. In fact, I've never introduced my family to anyone I've been with. Not even Elise, and I was with her for two years. Am I crazy to imagine Nicole sitting next to me at my parents' dinner table? Would she even want to?

I decide to let it go, for now. I don't want to overwhelm her again. I seem to be good at freaking her out. Truth be told, I'm starting to freak myself out.

"Tell you what," I say. "Spend the day with me. I'll make us some coffee and breakfast. We can go into town if we need to, or..." I trail my finger along her skin, tracing the outline of her breast. "We can stay here all day."

"That sounds perfect."

I think so, too.

16

RYAN

The day with Nicole is amazing. My only complaint is that it ends too soon. But skipping dinner with my family isn't an option, especially since my mom made a point to call me about it. Of course, she makes it a point to call me every time she wants me over for dinner. I guess the silver lining is I get a lot of home-cooked meals.

It's a while before I get up to make Nicole that breakfast and coffee I promised. The pink flush creeps across her cheeks and she bites her lip again. I'm defenseless against that look. I roll her around, playing with her, using my fingers and mouth. I make her squeal and giggle. It's hot as fuck. When I finally plunge my cock into her, we're both crazy with desire. I am not even kidding when I say I see stars when I come in her. Motherfucking stars. It's unbelievable.

I mention dinner at my parents' again, and she gives me that sweet little brow furrow. I can tell the idea stresses her out, so I tell her I'll miss her and ask if I can see her again tomorrow. That seems to relax her, and she says yes.

I don't want to wait until tomorrow to see her again. My

head is full of her as I drive to my parents' place, but family dinners with the Jacobsens aren't really in-and-out affairs. I'll probably be there late. Maybe I'll call her when I get home. I can text her and see if she answers.

My parents still live in the house where I grew up. Jetty Beach is a long sand spit, with the ocean on one side and the bay on the other. Our house is down near the south end, a big two story with a rooftop deck that overlooks the ocean. They bought the house when my mom was pregnant with my brother, wanting a place to raise their kids. Even now that their children are grown and gone, they seem to want to stay.

I pull into the driveway, noticing Cody's car already parked out front. I check the clock. Five fifty-nine. Good, I'm not late. I'm in such a good mood from my day with Nicole, I don't want anything screwing it up.

"Hey," I call out as I open the door.

"Hi, honey," my mom says from the kitchen.

I walk through the front room, with my mom's antique grandfather clock and comfortable but dated furniture. The back of the house is an open great room, with a kitchen, some seating, and a big farmhouse table lined with chairs. Mom stands at the stove, stirring. Her hair is about half gray and I don't think she's ever colored it in her life. Despite her old-fashioned tendencies, she dresses with a comfortable style. Her turquoise tunic flows down around a pair of slim jeans, matching turquoise sandals on her feet.

"Hi, Mom." I give her a kiss on the cheek and set down the bottle of her favorite Salishan Cellars wine I brought. "Can I help with anything?"

"I have this under control." She smiles at me over her shoulder. "How are you today?"

"I'm really good, actually." I can't very well tell her why, but I also can't wipe the grin off my face.

"You look good." She pauses her stirring and scrutinizes me with an intense gaze. "What's going on?"

I grab a tomato from the top of a salad and pop it in my mouth. "Nothing. You invited me to dinner. I'm here."

She raises one eyebrow at me.

"Is Dad up on the deck?" I need to get out of here before she starts an interrogation. To prevent her from asking more questions, I grab a beer out of the fridge and head for the stairs.

The deck covers the entire roof, a waist-high railing running around the perimeter. A built-in grill and stone counter sit on the side that overlooks the water. A big wicker sectional with blue-and-white striped cushions is set up nearby, and I see that my dad put up some new patio umbrellas to provide shade.

Cody and my dad stand over the grill, in classic man fashion. I notice there's no Jennifer lingering in the kitchen with my mom, and she isn't up here with Cody, either. I hope that means they're still broken up, or at least that she isn't coming tonight.

"Hey," Cody says, lifting his beer.

"Hey."

Dad has a line of steaks along the grill. My father is about six-one, an inch taller than me—although at six-two, Cody has us both beat. Dad keeps his gray hair shaved in a buzzcut, the same haircut he's gotten every three weeks for as long as I can remember. Today he wears a turquoise-and-blue Hawaiian shirt and a pair of khaki shorts. It's pretty warm for early spring, and when you live in a place that rains seventy percent of the year, a hint of sun tends to send us to our closets to dig out the shorts and sandals. I wonder if my mom coordinated their shirts; the colors match.

"Good evening, son," Dad says.

I walk over to do the customary inspection of the meat. "Hey, Dad. Those look good."

"Timing is everything." He sprinkles a little rock salt on the steaks. He has his grilling tools laid out in a neat row, and his spices set within reach. He takes his grilling very seriously.

I smile and take a swig of my beer. I lean against the built-in counter. Cody stares at me.

"What?" I ask.

"Huh," Cody says.

"What does that mean?"

My dad looks back and forth between the two of us and Cody shrugs at him. Dad turns his attention back to the steak.

You got laid, Cody mouths.

I give him the finger.

He nods his head in the direction of the railing. I scowl at him but follow him over. We both put our forearms on the rail, our beers dangling from our hands. The beach is two stories below us, grass-covered dunes leading to flat sand. Farther away, the waves roll in and out. It's low tide.

"Was it the girl I saw at your place the other day? Nicole?" Cody asks. "She was hot."

I clench my beer bottle. "Don't fucking talk about her."

"Whoa, dude," he says. "You don't have to go all sensitive artist on me. I was just asking."

"Why are you asking?" I don't know why I'm so defensive about it, but the way he called her hot irritates me.

"I don't know. You look different today. Better. I was just

wondering what's going on and if ... you know, if it's a good idea."

I'm getting tired of my family's scrutiny, but I kind of deserve it. I put them through a lot in the last year. "All right. Yes, it was Nicole. And hell if I know if it's a good idea. All I know is that she's amazing."

"Wow."

"Wow, what?"

Cody shrugs and takes a swig. "This is different than what I thought when I first saw you."

"Different?"

"Yeah. You didn't just get laid, did you?"

No, it was so much more than that. "Look, I don't really know what this is. She's great and I like her a lot. I'm..." I hesitate, looking out over the water, sparkling in the evening sun. "I'm happy. But I don't know if this is going to be a thing, or what. She lives in Seattle. She has a job there. It's not like we've been talking about the future. I'm just going to see what happens."

"All right. You tell Mom?"

"Fuck, no." I whirl on him and lower my voice. "Don't say anything. Seriously. I'm not even remotely ready for that right now. I'll punch you in the nuts."

"I won't say anything," he says with a laugh. "It's your thing. Just, do me a favor, okay?"

"What?"

"Be careful."

I turn back to the view and take a sip. I know he's right. My last relationship didn't just end with broken hearts. It was far worse.

"I'm okay, Cody, I swear. I'm in a good place."

"Good. Then I'm glad to see you happy. Really fucking glad, if I'm honest."

"Watch your mouth," Dad calls out over his shoulder.

"Sorry, Dad," Cody says.

"He heard every word we just said, didn't he?"

"Definitely. But you know he won't tell."

No, he won't. That's one of the great things about my dad. He hears more than he lets on, and he's basically the opposite of a gossip. He'll keep anything to himself, unless he thinks someone he loves is in danger.

I know that firsthand.

"So where's Jennifer?" I ask. "Anything going on with you guys?"

"I don't know. She says she wants to work it out."

"Do you think that's a good idea?"

"Probably not. I haven't really figured out what I'm going to do. Work is crazy right now. I've kind of been ignoring her."

"That's one way to deal with it."

He looks away and I can tell he doesn't want to talk about it. "Do you know why Mom invited us over? And why she insisted on doing this tonight?"

"No clue. I didn't say much to her when I came in."

"She gave you the interrogation look?"

"Yep."

"Don't blame you. But, pro tip: maybe wipe the grin off your face. You look suspicious."

I laugh. "Yeah, I don't think that's gonna happen."

We eat dinner on the deck at the slatted wood table my dad made. The sun dips low toward the water, and the waves keep up their steady rhythm. My dad is an absolute genius on the grill. My steak is cooked perfectly—medium rare, with just the right amount of pink, warm and tender throughout. It melts in my mouth.

Despite the delicious food, I have trouble keeping my

mind from wandering. I keep thinking about Nicole. I shift in my seat, trying not to imagine her naked body straddling me. I'm not very successful.

Mom casts a few looks in my direction, and I try to avoid her gaze without making it look like I'm avoiding her gaze. Cody talks about work, deflecting questions about Jennifer. Dad is characteristically reserved, but Mom doesn't say much either, which is unusual. It makes for an oddly quiet dinner at the Jacobsen house.

After we finish eating, Mom brings up lemon bars for dessert. She looks over her shoulder several times while I help her serve.

"Okay, Mom," Cody says. "What's going on?"

"Why would you think there's something going on? Ed." She looks at my dad. "Tell them there's nothing going on."

Dad doesn't say anything.

"You're acting weird," Cody says.

She takes her seat and picks up her fork. "I'm hardly acting weird."

"You actually are," I say. A new worry takes root. What if something is wrong? I can't believe I didn't think about it before. "Mom, are you sick? Dad?"

"No, no." She waves her hand. "We're fine."

"Then what *is* going on?" I ask.

"I think it's me."

We all turn around at the voice. It's Hunter.

"Oh, shit," Cody says under his breath.

Before I can stop myself, I fly out of my seat and stride over to Hunter. I have enough self-control to keep from punching him in the mouth—that will hurt me as much as him. But I ball my fist and slug him in the gut.

He doubles over, groaning. Good. I hope it hurts.

"Ryan!" My mom is right behind me, grabbing my arm to yank me back.

I pull away. "It's fine, Mom."

"It most certainly is *not* fine."

Hunter puts a hand up. "No," he says, his voice strained. He keeps an arm hugged to his stomach. "It's okay."

"What the fuck, Hunter?" Seeing him makes my blood burn with rage. Hunter disappeared the day after he graduated high school, leaving nothing but a vague note for my mother, telling her he was sorry. Six months later he sent a postcard, announcing that he'd enlisted in the Marines. Since then, my parents get a letter now and then, but otherwise none of us see or hear from him.

"Nine years," I say. "You left nine years ago, without a word to any of us. Am I supposed to be happy to see you?"

"Of course you should be happy to see him," Mom says. "Hunter is your brother, and we're thrilled to have him home."

I'm not done. "If he's our brother, why did he bail? He hasn't been here, Mom. He hasn't been here for anything." I turn back to Hunter. "Do you have any fucking idea what you missed? What we've been through? No, of course you don't. Because you didn't give a shit."

"Hey, Ryan," Cody says. "Take it down a notch, man. Let him talk at least."

"Great," I say, my voice thick with sarcasm. "Fine. Let's hear it, Hunter."

He stands tall, almost at attention. His brown hair is cut short in a military buzz, a striking contrast to the scruffy style that hung in his eyes when we were younger. He's dressed in civilian clothes, jeans and a polo, but carries himself with the unmistakable air of discipline you see in military men.

"He doesn't need to say anything right now." Mom grabs his hand and coaxes him toward the table. I wonder if she's worried he'll leave again and not come back. "Come on, Hunter. Sit down. Have you eaten yet?"

"So you knew," I say. "You knew he was coming and that's why we're here."

Mom scoots her seat to the table and passes the plate of fettuccine to Hunter. "Yes, I did know. Hunter told us he was coming and I wanted to surprise you both. I thought you'd be excited."

I take my seat and glance at Cody. He shrugs. Cody's too damn nice.

Hunter puts the pasta down, untouched. "Look, I owe all of you an explanation. I know that. Right now, all I can say is I'm sorry. I made a lot of mistakes. I probably can't ever make up for most of them, but I had to come back and at least give it a shot."

There's sincerity in his voice, but I'm too full of anger to look at him. He caused my mom so much hurt and worry.

"I'm going to go get another beer," I say.

I hear Cody follow me down the stairs, but I ignore him. My Nicole-induced glow is long gone. Even though I knew Hunter might be coming back, seeing him set me off. I go for the fridge, but I don't really want another beer. Burying my anger in alcohol is probably not a wise move.

"I think Mom underestimated how pissed you'd be," Cody says. "She should have told us he was coming."

"Would that have mattered?"

"Doubt it. I think she was worried we wouldn't come if we knew. You especially."

"Aren't you even a little pissed about this? We haven't seen him in nine years. What was I supposed to do, walk up and hug him?"

Cody shrugs. "I don't know. I guess I'd like to hear him out. Yeah, it's been a long time, but he's here now, right?"

I hunch my back and stare into the open fridge.

"Ryan." He pauses, and I know I'm not going to like what he says. I can hear it in his voice. "Is it possible you're pissed that he wasn't here when ... you know. He wasn't here for you, or for Mom when all the shit went down."

I take a deep breath. Cody has a point, whether or not I want to admit it. As much as Hunter put our mom through, I did worse. A lot worse. Maybe I'm still mad at myself, and seeing Hunter reminds me of it. Damn it. I don't want it to be my fault. I want to blame Hunter and hit him again.

"Yeah." I close the fridge door, my anger dissipating in the face of the truth. "I hate admitting when you're right."

Hunter emerges through the doorway to the stairs. Cody gestures him in and he joins us in the kitchen.

"Hey, man, I'm sorry I hit you," I say.

"It's all right. I deserved it." He rubs his stomach and winces. "I don't remember you being able to hit so hard."

"So, what, are you back now? Or is this just an appearance?"

He rubs his head. "I'm back. I'm out. Medical discharge."

Now that he mentions it, I can see he's walking with a bit of a limp.

"What happened?" Cody asks.

"It's a long story, but I fucked up my leg. I mean, I consider myself lucky. I know guys who lost limbs. It was brutal. At least I can still walk. But it was a career ender." He pauses, looking away. "Listen, Ryan—your mom told me things were rough for a while. I'm betting there's more she didn't say, but whatever it was, I should have been here. I'm sorry."

He holds out his hand. I step in and bat it aside, bringing

him in for a hug. We clap each other on the back and I move out of the way to let Cody hug him, too.

"It's good to have you back, man," I say. "I mean that."

Hunter looks around. "It's good to be back. More than I would have guessed."

I open the fridge again, pull out three beers, and hand them to Cody and Hunter. "Take one up to Dad. I'm good for tonight."

"Thanks, man," Cody says. "You coming back up?"

"Yeah, I gotta take a piss first."

They go back upstairs and I pull my phone out of my back pocket. I'm hoping I might have a text from Nicole. Maybe it's pathetic of me, but I miss her. Although it's good she wasn't here to see my little outburst. I stare at the screen, debating. Should I text her?

With a heavy exhale, I stick my phone back in my pocket. I'm falling for this girl way too hard and way too fast. I don't know if I'm up for this.

17

NICOLE

My bed in my old room feels so childish and small. And empty. I turn over and look at the clock. Nine-thirty. I'm surprised I slept so late. It took forever to fall asleep last night, my mind obsessively recalling the day I spent with Ryan. I can still smell him all over me. I think about texting him, but I'm terrified of coming on too strong. Sure, we had amazing sex, but that doesn't mean we're a couple. Does it? I feel so out of place.

Like I told Ryan already, navigating the world of adult singlehood is new to me. Is he waiting for me to call? Am I supposed to wait for him to call me? I think back to the last few romantic comedies I saw. Sweet as they were, I don't particularly want to mimic the bumbling struggles those characters always endure before they find love. I've had enough drama thrown at me recently, thank you very much. But my mind still reels with the implications of our day together.

Reluctantly, I drag myself out of bed. My parents are gone—they left a note on the fridge saying they're going into the city for the day. I'm just glad they didn't wake me. My mom relented on the coffee, as long as I promised to buy fair trade organic, so I start a pot. While I wait for it to brew, I get out my laptop, intending to catch up on some work.

I open my email and immediately close it again. Work. I need to go back. Working remotely is supposed to be temporary. I'm already stretching it, and if I don't show up in the office soon, I risk losing my job. The very thought of Seattle makes my stomach turn. That's where Jason is. Our apartment. The rest of my things.

The coffee finishes and I pour myself a cup. I have a friend from work, Andrea, who would probably let me crash at her place for a while. I'm certainly not going to stay at my old apartment. Even if Jason agreed to let me have it, I'd never be able to stay there. Damn him. He had sex with her right on top of my brand-new bedding. I'll never be able to look at that beautiful blue-and-silver comforter again.

And Ryan ... he's something I wasn't expecting. If I go back to Seattle, when will I see him? Weekends? Maybe we can switch off—he visits me one weekend, I come down here the next. Wait, what am I thinking? I can't start planning a long-distance relationship with this guy when I have no idea what is even happening between us. This isn't a relationship. Is it? This is ... I have no idea what this is.

I sip my coffee and tackle a few work tasks, trying to keep Ryan off my mind. Not like work is hard, even when I'm distracted. I add updated guest counts to a spreadsheet, send a few emails to vendors so they'll respond back early in the week, and check the status of a brochure order. Real brain surgery, there.

I deal with a few things for the festival as well. There isn't as much work as I feared, but I feel like this event is going to fall pretty flat. I went over Cheryl's lists, looked up photos of past events, and talked with a lot of the local businesses to see how it was done in the past. It isn't complicated, but it's also ... boring.

A bunch of tourists sporting fanny packs and white tennis shoes will wander around some booths. If the business owners are lucky, they'll go into their stores and spend money. Sure, the artists have a chance to sell their work, and it showcases a lot of great local talent. But there's no spark. Nothing to make it unique. Even the art gallery itself is *blah*. For a community that likes to pride itself on its artistic roots, they've really let this slide over the years. I wonder if there's anything I can do to spruce things up, even on such short notice.

My coffee's gone and I'm having a hard time concentrating. I keep thinking of Ryan. Remembering what he did with his tongue makes me all tingly. I was serious when I said it was my first time. Jason claimed oral sex grossed him out. The jackass was probably just too lazy to learn. I close my eyes, remembering how crazy Ryan drove me. Just thinking about it starts to get me wet.

I look at my phone again. Is he going to call? Is there a rule about how long you're supposed to wait?

Ryan's tongue gymnastics get me thinking. My inexperience with all things oral extends to performing it as well. I tried on Jason once, but it didn't go well. We were both uncomfortable and I don't think he enjoyed it any more than I did. But the thought of slipping Ryan's cock in my mouth is exhilarating. What does it taste like? I love the thought of making him feel good, of sending him into spasms of ecstasy the way he did for me. The problem is, I have no idea how.

I think about texting Melissa. But if I text, there will be a written record of our conversation. Instead, I bring up her number and hit send.

"Morning." She sounds tired.

"Did I wake you?"

"Nope, but I kind of wish you would have. I was up early grading tests."

"Sounds awesome."

"Eh, it's my life. What's up?"

I pause, biting my lower lip. Melissa isn't necessarily overly experienced, but she's dated more guys than I have. I figure she might be able to point me in the right direction. "So, I have a weird question."

"Oh-kay," she says, drawing out the word.

"How much do you know about blowjobs?"

I hear a snorting, choking sound, then coughing. "I'm sorry, you just made me spit water everywhere. What did you say?"

"Geez, Mel, you heard me."

"I think I heard you. Did you just ask me about blowjobs? Oh my god. You did it, didn't you? You fucked Ryan."

"Shh." I glance around, although I know there isn't anyone in the house.

"What, is your mom around?"

"No, they're gone for the day."

"Then what are you so worried about? Come on, Nicole, you're a grown woman. And my god, you deserved a good fuck. It was good, wasn't it?"

I pause. "It was incredible."

Melissa squeals. "I knew it! How was the Brazilian? Awesome, right? I told you."

My face warms, but I couldn't stop smiling if I tried. "I didn't think I'd ever be thanking you for that epic torture session, but yes. It was awesome."

"Okay, so what happens now? You want to blow him; that's a good sign."

"I have no idea. I haven't talked to him yet. He had to leave last night to go have dinner with his parents, but holy shit Melissa, we had sex pretty much all day. It was unbelievable."

Melissa groans. "I'm so jealous."

"So, what do I do? He did all this crazy stuff, and I swear to you, I had no idea half of it was even possible. I don't want to disappoint him, you know?"

"You're adorable. Okay, here's what you're going to do," she says, using her teacher voice. "You're going to Google *how to give a sexy blowjob* and—"

"Wait, what? No."

"No, what?"

"I'm not Googling *how to give a blowjob*."

"Why not?"

"Because!" Doesn't she know anything?

"You're afraid someone will find out, aren't you?"

"If I type that in, who knows who could see it. What if someone finds my search history?"

"What if they do?"

"Seriously? What would they think?"

"Um, they'd think you're a grown ass woman who wants to blow a man's mind by sucking his cock. I'd say they'd probably be impressed and maybe ask you out."

"Shut up, Simon."

"Look, Nic, there are a lot of really good articles out there explaining how to do this stuff. You know how tribal women would have lived close to their moms and sisters and aunts? They would learn from their elders, and it wasn't just how to gather berries and roots and shit. They'd learn all the good stuff too, like how to properly suck a cock. The internet is like our modern-day women's circle. You can learn from the best—it doesn't have to be weird."

"I guess when you put it that way..."

"Do it. The internet police aren't going to come arrest you if you Google cock sucking. But maybe don't phrase it like that."

I laugh. "Okay, okay. I'll do it."

"And Nicole?"

"Yeah?"

"Let me know how it goes."

"Shut up, Simon."

I hang up on her.

With a deep breath, I open a browser and type *how to give a sexy blowjob*. I hesitate, my mouse hovering over the search icon. What am I so afraid of? I *am* a grown ass woman, and hell yes, I want to blow a man's mind by sucking his cock. I click the button.

MY PHONE BINGS and I nearly jump out of my seat. I clap a hand to my chest and blow out a breath. That scared me. I pick it up and my heart skips again. A text from Ryan.

Hey. Are you busy?

I glance up at the clock on the microwave. It's after one o'clock. Where did the morning go?

My fingers hover above the tiny keyboard on the screen. What should I say? I don't want to sound too eager. That might scare him off. But I'm already pretty turned on by the research I've been doing, and just the thought of seeing him again makes my tummy flutter. *Oh, come on, Nicole. Type something. If you wait too long, he's going to think you don't want to talk to him.*

I send a reply. *Nope, not busy.*

I groan and slump in my seat. The epitome of conversation, that.

Instead of *bing*ing with another text, my phone rings. I can't keep the smile from my face as I answer.

"Hi."

"Hi, beautiful."

Oh my god. "Um, hi."

He laughs. "Sorry, I texted first to make sure I wasn't interrupting anything important."

Nope, just learning how to blow your mind. "No, not at all. I'm just hanging out here at my parents' house."

"Can I come pick you up?"

"Yes." *Ugh, I said it too quickly.*

"Great. I'll see you in a little bit."

"Okay, see you then."

I hang up, my eyes lingering on the article I was reading. He didn't say why he was coming to get me. Is this going to be a date? A hook-up? Heat is already building between my legs. What is he doing to me? I don't have long before he'll arrive, but I haven't showered, so I decide to rinse off. I can just put my hair up. I dash into the bathroom to get ready, wondering what he has in store for me. And what I have in store for him.

18

RYAN

It took all my self-control not to call Nicole after I left my parents' house. But my mom kept us there late; it was well after midnight by the time Cody and I left. Nicole was probably asleep.

This morning, I keep holding back. I want to see her so much it's painful, but the intensity of my reaction scares me. I don't want to ride this high too far—it will only make the crash back down that much harder. And longer. I need to be careful, but by about one o'clock I can't take it anymore. She hasn't called me either, but I'm done waiting.

I race down the highway to town after talking to her. I already showered and dressed in jeans and a faded blue t-shirt, so I'm out the door in seconds. I'm not going to just bring her back to my place. This isn't a booty call. Of course, I'm hard just thinking about her, and we'll certainly end up back at my place if I have anything to say about it. Still, I should take her out. Maybe lunch if she hasn't eaten. Can I sit across a table from her and control myself? Of course I can.

Maybe.

I pull up to her house and lift my hand to knock on the door. She opens it before I finish knocking.

"Hi," she says, a little breathless. Her hair is wet, as if she's just gotten out of the shower, and she's put it up in a little bun. She wears a long-sleeved black shirt and a red-and-white skirt that shows a lot of leg.

Lunch will take too long. We'll get coffee. To go.

"Hi." I step in and slip my hand around her waist, pulling her to me. Her lips part in a smile and I lean in, kissing her. She offers no resistance, tilting her head for me. Her mouth is soft and minty. I mean to give her a quick hello kiss, but I linger there, breathing in her scent. Her tongue brushes my lips and I pull her closer, wrapping my other hand around the back of her neck.

Forget the coffee. Is her house empty?

I break the kiss, pulling back to look at her. "It's good to see you."

"You too. "So, what are we going to do?"

Baby, the things I'm going to do to you. Still, I find myself saying, "I thought we could grab lunch."

"Sounds great."

There's a hint of nervousness about her as I walk her to my car. Or maybe it's anticipation. I hold the door and watch her legs as she sits. Her skirt slides higher up her thigh. She definitely wore it to torture me. Her pale, creamy skin looks so soft and inviting.

I shut her door and get in the car. She gives me a shy smile, like she has a secret.

"What sounds good?" I ask, pulling out of her driveway.

"I'm fine with whatever."

I glance down at her legs again and she tips her knees apart, ever so slightly. I can't stop myself from touching her

—I run my fingers up her thigh, swirling it near the hem of her skirt.

Nicole takes a deep breath. "Actually, I have another idea."

"Yeah? All right, just tell me where to go." My fingers tingle as I caress her skin and my cock strains against my jeans. I can't believe I get to be the one to touch her like this.

"This might be a little crazy. Have you ever gone up Forest Hill Road?"

I raise my eyebrows. Is she serious? "I've, um, I've driven up there, but never with a girl." Forest Hill Road is an old logging road outside town. It winds through the regrown forest to a secluded hill. Many a Jetty Beach teenager lost their virginity on Forest Hill—or at least claimed they did.

She reaches over and runs her hand up my leg, getting dangerously close to my cock. "So this would be a first for you?"

"Yeah," I say, a little shaky. "Forest Hill would be a first."

"Good." She moves her hand over my bulge and squeezes through my jeans.

I groan and grip the steering wheel, my other hand still on her leg. Nicole leans across the center console and undoes my jeans, sliding the zipper down. Holy shit, is this happening? Did Nicole Prescott just ask me to take her up to Forest Hill? I'm so turned on, my cock feels like it will burst, and her delicate caresses make my whole body light up with electricity.

"Oh my god, Nicole, what are you doing to me?"

Her hand slides into my underwear. She wraps her fingers around my cock and squeezes.

I blow out a breath and try to focus on the road. A few cars amble by as I drive through town. Fucking speed limit. I press on the gas pedal, testing my luck a little bit. This is not a good time to get pulled over, but fuck me, I need to get on the highway.

We turn past the town entrance and I'm able to pick up speed. So does Nicole. She pulls my cock out and strokes her hand up and down the shaft. I run my hand higher up her thigh, beneath her skirt, my fingers brushing lace. She scoots closer to me and opens her legs. I tease my fingers beneath her panties.

"You're so wet."

My blood is on fire, but I have to keep my eyes on the road. Nicole keeps stroking me, putting pressure in all the right places. She swirls her thumb over the tip and I almost swerve off the road.

"Sorry."

I slide two fingertips inside her and she moans, squeezing my cock harder.

Where's that fucking turn?

"Is that it?" Nicole asks, using her free hand to point to a gravel road on the left.

"God, I hope so."

I turn and the car bounces along the uneven surface. Nicole glances behind us, then looks at me, biting her lower lip.

She unlatches her seat belt and leans down, putting her head in my lap. Her tongue circles the tip of my cock. My eyes go blurry and the car bounces. I put a hand on her head to keep her from hitting the steering wheel.

"Holy shit, Nicole."

She slides me into her mouth, her tongue warm and slick. She sucks in a little and I groan, trying desperately to keep the car on the gravel. The road is so uneven, I have to slow down. She takes the shaft in her hand and pulls while she works the tip with her mouth.

"Fuck me, Nicole, that feels amazing. I don't think I can keep driving if you do that."

In answer, she takes more of me into her mouth, and draws out again.

"Oh my god." I press on the brake and stop. I'm going to hit a tree if I keep going.

She moves her mouth up and down, sucking on the crown when she gets to the top. I lean my head back, breathing hard. Her every move makes me shudder. I fist my hand through her hair, careful not to push her down, letting her lead. I want to put my fingers inside her, to make her feel this way too, but I can't think clearly. Her body is angled too far for me to reach her pussy, so I ease the seat back to make sure she has room, and enjoy the feel of her mouth on me.

Is this actually happening? Did Nicole Prescott just take me up Forest Hill Road to suck my cock? It's like all my craziest teenage fantasies come true. Except I never even thought to fantasize about this—it would have seemed impossible. So far out of reach, it was too stupid to use as jack off material. But fuck me if it isn't happening.

Even if I had fantasized about it before, it never would have been this good in my imagination.

The tension builds, and she keeps going. I'm going out of my mind, but I'm not sure if she wants me to come in her mouth.

"Whoa, Nicole." I'm practically panting. "God, that's so good. That's..." She does something with her tongue and I rock my head back against the seat and groan. "You better slow down, baby."

She swivels her head just a little and I look down. Those big, blue eyes look up at me, her lips pursed around the tip of my cock. It is the hottest motherfucking thing I've ever seen in my entire life: Nicole looking up at me with my dick in her mouth. My muscles clench and I almost come right there.

I let out a breath and put my fingers beneath her chin. "Come up here."

She plunges down on my cock one last time and I groan again. As unbelievable as this is, I want to be inside her. She sits up and wipes her hand across her chin.

"Did you like that?" The hint of worry in her voice is the cutest thing.

"Are you kidding? You just blew my mind."

A wide smile spreads across her face. I adjust the seat back again and grab her, pulling her on top of me. She straddles over my lap, her hot little skirt pulling up over her legs. I reach under and push my fingers inside her, rubbing her clit. She makes delicious little noises as I move. I grab the firm flesh of her ass with one hand while the other plays with the soft, wet skin between her legs.

"Ryan, stop teasing me," she says, trying to push her hips down. "I want your cock in me."

Of course that means I have to tease her a little more, but my cock throbs at her proximity.

"Tell me again what you want."

"I want you inside me."

How can I deny a request like that?

I push her panties to the side and grab her hips, lowering her onto me. I slide in with ease, feeling the hot, sweet pressure envelop me. My eyes roll back and I clutch at her ass, moving her back and forth.

"This was such a good idea," I say.

She lets out a breathy giggle. Her thighs squeeze against me as she rocks her hips up and down. I slip my hands up her shirt and beneath her bra, feeling her hard nipples. She picks up the pace, riding me harder. Fuck me, I'm going to come too fast. She got me so close with her mouth already.

"Careful, baby," I say. "This is too good."

"No, don't hold back."

I can feel her getting hotter, her muscles clenching around me. I grab her ass, picking her up so she can slide back down. My orgasm builds, the pressure almost torture.

"Oh my god, Ryan. You feel amazing."

I grip her hips, slowing her down. "Look at me."

Nicole meets my eyes, her breath coming fast. We pause, both on the brink of climax. I stare, devouring every inch of her. Those sparkling blue eyes, that sweet, delicious mouth.

She rolls her hips, grinding herself into me. My mouth drops open. She moans, repeating the motion.

"Are you ready?" I ask.

"Yes."

I guide her hips, pushing her back and forth. She slides up and down my cock, sending jolts of pleasure through me. She speeds up, crying out, and throws her head back. Her pussy clenches around me and her orgasm triggers mine. My cock pulses inside her, bursting with waves of pleasure. My mind goes blank. Nothing exists except us, this moment, this feeling.

When we both finish, she slumps against me. I wrap my arms around her, burying my face in her neck.

"That was unreal," I say.

She pulls back to look at me. Her hair is tousled and her cheeks flushed. "Yeah, it was."

I lean forward to kiss her.

As if coming back to herself, she looks around and laughs. The windows are so foggy, we can't see through them. "I can't believe I just did that."

"That makes two of us." I kiss her forehead, her nose, her

lips. I'm euphoric, enjoying my post-orgasm glow. I think about cooking dinner for her later. If the weather holds out, we can make a fire on the beach.

Nicole moves off my lap back into the passenger seat. I adjust my pants and zip them up. She smooths her skirt down and shifts sideways to look at me.

"So, um, that was incredible," she says.

I blow out a breath. "That's the understatement of the century. To be clear, this isn't exactly what I meant when I said I'd come pick you up. Not that I'm complaining."

She laughs. "I know. I've never done anything like this before. You make me feel so brave, like I can take chances. And I thought it would be fun to surprise you."

"That was definitely a surprise."

She smiles again, but her eyes drop and her face turns serious. "Ryan, the last couple days have been amazing. I'm not sure what this is, or where it's going, or if we're even supposed to have a conversation about that yet."

"Don't get so hung up on 'supposed to.' There's no rule book we have to follow."

"Fair enough. I guess I need to know what this is to you. I can't stay in Jetty Beach. I have to get back to my job or I'm probably going to get fired."

My euphoria flees in an instant. I knew she wasn't planning to stay in town with her parents forever, but this takes me by surprise. "When are you leaving?"

"Tomorrow. I won't get back in time to go into the office, but I can at least figure out where I'm going to stay. Maybe grab more of my stuff from my apartment. I have a meeting on Tuesday that I really should attend, and we have a luncheon on Friday. I can't exactly help with an event from here."

"Yeah, of course. That makes sense."

"So, I was wondering... do you want me to come down next weekend? Or was this sort of ... I don't know. Temporary?"

I meet her eyes and reach out to touch her cheek. "I would love for you to come down next weekend. You can stay at my place if you want."

Her smile cuts through the sense of foreboding that threatens to disturb my happiness. We can make this work. I don't like the hollow feeling in my chest, but I tell myself I'm just taken aback by her leaving. She'll do what she has to do for her job, and I'll see her soon. She'll be fine. I know that.

I'm not so sure about me.

19

RYAN

I should have seen my relapse coming. I know the signs—what to look for. But that's the thing about depression. It sneaks in and waits, hiding in the shadows. When it senses weakness, it doesn't pounce. Instead of hitting hard and fast, out in the open, it slithers in through the cracks. It lodges itself in your vulnerable places and takes root. Before you know it, you're slogging through its depths, and it can be hard as fuck to pull yourself out.

Nicole leaves for Seattle the next day, assuring me she has a place to stay with a friend from work. I think about driving up with her, maybe staying the week. I have a shoot on Wednesday, but I can reschedule.

In the end, I hold back. We shared a couple of amazing days together, but I'm rushing. I'm falling for her headlong, and when I crash back to Earth, it's going to hurt. Better to keep my distance and let her go. I'll see her in a week. After that, we'll see what happens.

Tuesday dawns and I stay in bed half the morning. Getting up doesn't seem too important, so I don't bother. My brother calls and I ignore him for a few hours before finally calling him back. I don't answer when my mom tries to call me either, but I text her to say I'm busy and I'll talk to her tomorrow.

The days go on like that, and weeks go by. I don't sleep well at night and spend my days tired and irritable. Nicole comes down every weekend. I offer to come up and see her, but she's rooming with a friend and says it won't be very comfortable to have me stay there. She also turns down my offer of booking a hotel. I respect that, although I feel guilty that she has to do all the driving.

Still, I live for weekends. I shuffle through life during the week, knowing that as soon as she shows up at my door, I'll feel better. I'll feel alive again.

And I do. We watch movies, take naps, eat out, and make sweet, hot, exquisite love—on my bed, on the floor, in the studio. Even once on the beach, although it's cold as shit. Afterward, we take a hot shower together and decide maybe that's an experience best not repeated.

And every Sunday night, she packs her duffel bag, gets in her car, and drives away. Back to her life.

There's no way this is going to last.

It pisses me off that I'm so despondent over her. I shouldn't need another person, even a person as incredible as Nicole, to make me want to get out of bed in the morning. How did I survive before I met her? I was doing well. I bought the church, worked hard on renovations, kept my business going. I traveled to shoots on location, and took on new clients when my studio was finished. My parents invited me to dinner at least once a week, and it didn't seem like a chore to go visit.

After Nicole has been gone a few weeks, I find myself spending long days on my couch playing *Halo*. I look up at the clock and realize I spent an entire day just sitting, doing nothing. And the worst part is, I don't really care.

Late on a Thursday night, I get a text from Nicole. I hardly spoke to her all week. She had an event at work and she put in long hours getting everything ready.

Hey, event is done! Went great. Boss gave me tomorrow off. Mind if I come early?

It should make me happy. I should be excited at the thought of seeing her tomorrow, instead of waiting until Saturday. We'll have three days together, instead of two. Isn't that good news?

Then why do I stare listlessly at my phone, not sure what to say?

Sounds great.

Yay! I'll get up early so I can be with you sooner.

I figure I should reply, but I feel like the emptiness is eating me alive. I toss my phone back on the couch and stretch my legs out. Have I eaten dinner today? I have no idea. I don't really care.

"Hey, sleepyhead."

Nicole's voice rouses me and I turn over. I was sleeping in my clothes. I rub my eyes and blink at her. "What time is it?"

"Ten. Are you okay?"

"Yeah, just overslept. How was the drive?"

"Amazingly, not bad," she says, sitting down on the edge of the bed. "I figured traffic would be terrible on a Friday morning, but I guess I got lucky."

I sit up, still feeling groggy. I was awake, staring at the ceiling, until at least four last night. "Good."

"Are you okay?"

No. I'm sinking. Don't believe what I say. "Yeah, I'm fine. Sorry, I just had trouble sleeping last night. I could use some coffee."

"Well, you're in luck." She gets up and walks over to a table and grabs two coffees. "I picked these up on the way. They're still pretty hot."

I take the brown cup with the Old Town Café logo on the side. I smile at her, because it seems like what I should do.

"You can take your time, but I figured we could go into town later. I need to turn in the event permits for the festival, and since I'm here on a weekday, I thought I could do it in person."

"Okay."

She narrows her eyes at me. "Are you sure you're all right?"

The concern in her voice cuts through my haze. "Yeah, I'm sorry Nicole. I haven't been getting enough sleep." I stand and slip a hand around her waist, pulling her close. "I missed you."

"Mm, I missed you too," she says between kisses. "This is more like it."

WE SPEND the day in town. Working with her on festival business makes me feel slightly less useless. She chats with a few shop owners, talking about ideas for sprucing up their outdoor decor. She smiles and laughs, and is personable and sweet. It takes a lot of energy for me to engage with people. After an hour, I want nothing more than to go back home and sack out on my couch. But Nicole has enough enthusiasm for both of us, and by the afternoon I simply follow along, hoping she'll be finished soon.

"I'm starving," she says after talking to the owner of the florist shop for what seems like hours. "Want to get some food?"

"I guess." The thought of sitting in a restaurant is strangely abhorrent. "Why don't we just go back to my place? We can get something to eat there."

"I think you might have a half-eaten bag of pretzels and some beer at your place, but that's about it."

A spike of irritation runs through me. "Well, you showed up here a day early. What am I supposed to do? Keep my fridge stocked in case you decide to come by on a whim?"

She looks at me with her mouth open. "Seriously? What's wrong with you?"

"Nothing." I know I'm being short with her and she's done absolutely nothing to deserve it, but that only makes me angrier. "I just don't want to go to a fucking restaurant right now."

"Great. Do I get asshole Ryan this weekend? I'm so glad I decided to come for an extra day."

She stomps back to my car and gets in the passenger side. I get in and start the car, refusing to look her direction. From the corner of my eye, I see her sitting with her arms crossed, her legs angled away from me.

We drive to my house in silence. What the hell is wrong with her, anyway? I didn't ask her to come today. For all she knew, I have work to do. Does she expect me to just drop everything because she has a day off?

When we pull up the driveway, she flies out of the car almost before I stop. I don't get out. What is wrong with me? Why am I convincing myself I'm mad at her? I don't have anything to be mad about.

"Fuck!" I beat my fist against the steering wheel. I'm such an asshole.

Nicole comes charging out of the studio, her bag in hand. She fumbles with her keys, throws open her car door and tosses her bag inside.

I lurch out of my car in a panic. I can't let her go like this. "Wait, Nicole. Please."

She stops, her back to me, her hand on her car door.

I walk over to stand behind her. I'm close enough to touch her but I don't dare. "I'm sorry. Really, I'm so sorry. That was all me. I don't know what's wrong with me lately. Please don't go."

She slowly turns to face me. "What's going on with you? Every time I drive down, I don't know who I'll see when I get here. Will it be sweet, sensitive Ryan? Will he kiss my fingertips and tell me how much he missed me? Or will it be grumpy, asshole Ryan, the guy who snaps at me for no reason and can't be bothered to get out of bed in the morning."

"I know, you're right. I get like this sometimes. It's stupid. I'm sorry. It isn't your fault."

"You need to just tell me if you're feeling bad," she says. "I can see it, you know. I'm not blind."

I step closer and brush her hair back from her face. "I know you're not. You're amazing and wonderful and I don't deserve you." *No, I don't. Not today, not tomorrow. Not ever.* I close my eyes and brush my lips against her cheek. "Please don't leave."

She leans her mouth close to my ear. "All right. I'll go inside with you. Then you have five minutes to convince me to stay."

She nibbles on my earlobe, and my dick stirs. I'll have to do my best.

20

NICOLE

The sound of the keynote speaker fills the room, but I have no idea what he's saying. He's some bigwig from Microsoft. Or he was. I'm not quite sure, since I find it more or less impossible to focus on what he's saying. My mind is in a million other places, rather than in the large hotel conference room.

I'm working, but there isn't much left for me to do. The charity lunch seems to be going well. Table assignments are done. Programs have been passed out. The hotel caterer set up on time, and the menu was followed. The low buzz of conversation filled the room while well-dressed executives networked, gossiped, and prepared to donate to the cause of the week. For a second, I can't remember what this lunch is for. I look down at the clipboard in my hands. A youth organization. Good. This is good. Meaningful. It's a worthy way to spend my time.

I sigh and lean against the check-in table at the back of the room. I'm grateful it's Friday. The last couple of months have felt like leading a double life, and it's starting to wear on me. I moved in with my co-worker, Andrea, renting the tiny extra bedroom in her condo. It's nice of her to let me stay, and the temporary arrangement suits me. She doesn't need me to sign a lease, just pay her month to month until I find a new place. I looked up a few potential apartments online, but between work during the week and spending my weekends with Ryan, I haven't made much progress on actually finding somewhere else to live.

I picked up the last of my things at my old apartment. It was so surreal. Jason at least kept his promise to be away. He also made no effort to hide the fact that another woman lives there. The pink bottle of hand lotion next to the kitchen sink, the stylish cream-colored trench coat hanging by the door, the new throw pillows on the couch. Maybe that should bother me, but it doesn't. I feel strangely at peace.

Someone had put my clothes in a large suitcase, and two moving boxes waited near the door, my name scrawled across them in Jason's handwriting. I stood in the center of the apartment, looking around. It still had the same furniture, pieces Jason and I had bought together. I didn't want any of it. I probably could argue to get half, or at least push to split up some of what we amassed over the years. But none of it felt like mine. It was as if it belonged to another girl—a girl who'd lived a pretend life.

After loading up the boxes in the back of my car, and throwing the suitcase in the trunk, I left. I contemplated tossing the boxes unopened, but they probably contained a few mementos I'd like to keep. And just like that, I closed the book on a story I thought I'd written perfectly when I was seventeen: Girl meets boy. They fall in love. They navigate the trials of early adulthood, get college degrees, start successful and lucrative careers, get engaged, throw a grand wedding, buy a house in the suburbs with a picket fence.

It was a nice fantasy. But it wasn't real.

The speaker apparently makes a good point because the audience claps while he pauses. I flip the papers on my clipboard to the back where I slipped in my to-do list for the Jetty Beach Art Festival. The event is still a few weeks away, and I think I have most of it under control. I have to admit, I'm pleased with myself, and the lack of a real committee has given me a lot of creative freedom. I ordered new banners to replace the old, fraying ones. A graphic designer friend of mine whipped up a great design with a new logo. I have them in the trunk of my car, and I can't wait to bring them down and show them to some of the business owners. I talked the city into letting me block off traffic to the main plaza downtown so we can set up more tents, and I recruited food trucks to come in for the weekend. Ryan arranged for street performers and a great little local band to come play, and worked with the local shop owners on sprucing up their storefronts with hanging flower baskets and potted plants. All in all, it's shaping up to be a great weekend.

"I feel like I've heard this speech before."

The man's voice startles me and I inadvertently gasp.

"Sorry," he says, leaning close so he can speak quietly. "I didn't mean to scare you."

"No, it's fine." I nearly gasp again when I see who it is. Jackson Bennett. I've seen him at a few events over the years, but even if I'd never seen him in person, I would know who he is. He's famous, at least in the Seattle area. A local executive, he has a reputation for being a rich playboy. Really rich, apparently, the type that begins with a *B*. A few months ago, he was on the cover of Seattle Weekly as the Pacific Northwest's most eligible bachelor.

"This is a nice event, don't get me wrong," he says. "But you attend enough of them, and they all start to seem the same. I keep threatening to just mail in my check, but my assistant claims it's important to be seen."

I laugh, glancing at him from the corner of my eye. He's dressed in an impeccable pair of dark gray slacks and a pale blue button-down shirt—no tie, the collar open. He has dark hair and piercing blue eyes. I'm certainly not about to get flirtatious with him, but I can still appreciate a good-looking man for what he is. And this one is something else.

"That seems to be the way the game is played. Being seen."

He puts his hands in his pockets. "I get tired of it sometimes."

"I can understand that," I say. "At least, I understand what it's like to be tired of going through the motions of your life, mostly because you think that's what other people expect of you."

Jackson grins. "Yeah, exactly. What are you doing after this?"

His question catches me so off guard I almost gasp again. "I, um... No, I have to wrap things up here, and I have a long drive ahead of me in the morning. Plus, I'm not available. In general."

He gives me an easy smile and nods. "No, I'm sure you're not. Sorry, I had to ask. I don't mean to be rude."

"No, it's fine. Thank you anyway."

"So now that we've established I won't hit on you," he says, "where are you headed on your long drive?"

Wow, he's just going straight for personal, isn't he? Yet his stance is so casual, his manner so easygoing, I find myself answering. "Jetty Beach. It's a little town out on the coast. I grew up there, and my, um, reason for not being available is there."

Jackson winces. "Long-distance relationship? Ouch. I tried that once. It ... yeah, it didn't turn out so well."

"It has its challenges."

"Sorry. My reputation for being a jackass is pretty credible. I'm told some people have this thing called a social filter and they don't actually say everything that comes to mind. I don't think I was born with one."

"That's all right."

"So, Jetty Beach. I spent a summer down there when I was a kid."

"Did you? It's a nice town. I kind of thought I was over it when I moved away to go to college. But it's actually quite sweet. I'm helping them put on their annual art festival in a few weeks. I think it will be a nice event."

Why am I telling him all this? It isn't like he asked. I guess it's refreshing to chat with someone without worrying they're going to have a sudden mood change. Ryan has been so strange the last few weekends—sweet one minute, grumpy the next. I'm never sure what I'm going to get when I see him. Still, it doesn't excuse talking Jackson Bennett's ear off about something I'm sure he has no interest in. Maybe *my* filter isn't working.

"Art festival, huh," Jackson says. "When is it?"

"It starts on the fifteenth."

"I haven't been out there in years. Maybe I'll have to come down."

Is he still hitting on me? A man like Jackson Bennett might not be too worried about whether a woman says she isn't available. But he says it with such a nonchalant air, maybe he just wants to visit the beach.

"Sure, that would be great. Although, don't expect too much. It's a small town, and a small-town festival. The art gallery is supposed to be the center of the festival, and it's gotten pretty run down. The owner just retired last year, and I don't think anyone has been taking good care of the building."

"Huh," he says. "Is it for sale? Maybe I'll buy it."

I glance at him and must have a confused look on my face. One corner of his mouth turns up in a smirk.

"Here," he says, pulling a business card and handing it to me. "Send me the details."

He smiles—he really is easy on the eyes—and wanders back to the luncheon. I tuck his business card in my clipboard, wondering if I'll have the guts to call him. He has an email address at the bottom. Maybe I'll just email him.

But my thoughts are already spinning. An outside investor would be a huge boon for Jetty Beach. If someone like Jackson Bennett came in and started redevelopment and revitalization projects, it could bring in a lot more business. I'll have to put some thought into how to approach it, but maybe my random conversation with Seattle's Most Eligible Bachelor can turn into something productive.

I glance at the time on my phone. Another half hour. The keynote speaker finishes his talk, and the audience starts in with a polite round of applause. Next, they'll get their checkbooks out or fill out donation slips with their credit card information. Some more mingling, sipping of drinks, and back to their offices they'll go. I'll have my work cut out for me, entering their donation information into the database and processing their thank-you letters. It's time consuming and tedious, more busywork than anything. I swear, sometimes I feel like a monkey could do my job.

I hope I can cut out of work a little early once things are wrapped up here. I think about doing some apartment hunting, but I can't find any motivation. Signing a lease will mean making the weekly drive back and forth to the beach a more or less permanent situation. But what else am I supposed to do? My job is here. I'm trying to rebuild a life. I honestly don't know how Ryan fits into that, long-term. I miss him terribly during the week. I live for the weekends. But how long can this last?

I know the strain is getting to him too. As much as I want to ignore the signs, his increasing moodiness is impossible to ignore. We've only been together a couple of months. Maybe he's growing tired of the back and forth.

A hollow pit opens up in my stomach at the thought of breaking things off with Ryan. I don't want that. I'm crazy about him. I thought I was in love with Jason all those years, but looking back, I realize I was never in love. A teenage crush had simply dragged on too long. Way too long. But Ryan—am I in love with him? My heart beats harder just thinking about him and I think about hopping in my car after work and braving the Friday traffic to get to him sooner. I don't want to wait until morning.

I don't know if it's love. Or maybe I'm afraid to admit that it is. But I know it's something worth fighting for.

21

NICOLE

It's sweet Ryan who greets me late that night when I finally pull up to his house. He meets me at the door with a glass of red wine and a big chocolate brownie. We barely make it inside before we're tearing our clothes off. He bends me over the velvet chaise, grabbing my hips tight while he pounds into me. I've been so stressed, I want it hard and fast, and he certainly gives it to me. Afterward, we get crumbs all over his couch eating the brownie and finishing off the bottle of wine. I fall asleep tangled in his arms, more than a little drunk, and happier than I've been in a while.

The next morning, I gather some courage and fire off an email to Jackson Bennett. I remind him we spoke at the luncheon, and give him the details about the art festival and a little information about the art gallery, as well as the town. I don't expect to hear back from him, but figure it's worth a shot. Ryan makes us breakfast, and we eat and sip coffee.

An open window brings in a fresh breeze. Ryan taps his finger against the countertop. It looks like he's staring into space.

I sidle up behind him and lean my cheek against his back. "What's wrong?"

"What? Nothing. Sorry. Just ... something I want to talk to you about."

My chest constricts and I freeze. He sounds so serious. It worries me.

"Okay," I say, trying very hard to sound normal.

"My parents invited me to dinner tonight," he says, turning around. "Would you come meet my family?"

Relief washes over me and I smile. "Yes, I'd love to meet your family."

He lets out a heavy sigh. "Good. I'm sorry, this is a big deal for me. I've never brought anyone home to meet them before."

That's surprising. I know he had one long-term relationship before. He never introduced her to his family? I wonder why, but I'm not going to ask.

"Should I be nervous?" I ask. "All of a sudden I'm nervous."

Ryan smiles, his dimples puckering beneath his stubble. "No, of course not. My mom can be chatty, and she'll probably ask me inappropriate questions in front of you. There might even be baby pictures." He laughs, shaking his head. "Come to think of it, I'm the one who should be nervous. You have nothing to worry about."

"Are you sure?"

"Positive. They're going to love you just as much as I do."

My eyes widen and I pull away. Did he just say...

Ryan clears his throat and walks into the kitchen. He turns the faucet on and washes off our dishes. I decide to let his comment go. I feel like I'm treading on thin ice with him so much lately, and don't want to ruin his good mood. But he did almost say it, didn't he?

He rinses off his hands and dries them on a towel, his dimples standing out with his half grin. "You know what? I have an idea."

"Yeah?"

"Follow me."

He leads me out into the studio and picks up one of his cameras.

"What's that for?" I ask.

"It takes pictures."

I smack him on the arm. "I know it takes pictures. What does this have to do with me?"

"I want to take pictures of you."

I bite my lip again. "What sort of pictures?"

"All sorts. I won't do anything you aren't comfortable with. It doesn't even have to be boudoir shots, although I can do that if you want me to. All this time I've had the most beautiful model I can imagine, and I've never taken your picture."

"I didn't bring any good clothes or anything."

He brushes my hair back from my face. "That's okay. I want you just like this. The real you."

HE TAKES me down to the beach—fully dressed. There's a light breeze, cool without being freezing. The sun shines overhead and the sky is blue all the way to the horizon. Standing on the flat sand makes the sky seem to stretch on forever. I have on a pair of boyfriend jeans with the cuffs rolled up and a loose-knit beige sweater with a white tank underneath. They don't seem like photography-worthy clothes, but Ryan assures me I look perfect.

For a while we just walk. He carries his camera and takes

a few shots of the ocean. He turns around once to shoot our footsteps. But for the most part, we wander, our bare feet sinking into the sand.

At some point I realize Ryan isn't beside me. I stop and look over my shoulder to find him pointing the camera at me.

He lowers the camera and looks down at the screen. "Don't worry about what I'm doing. Just enjoy a nice walk on the beach."

I smile and keep walking. He catches up and runs around me, taking pictures from different angles. A few times he asks me to stop, but he never has me pose. The wind blows my hair back and I fret about how little makeup I'm wearing, but Ryan seems to be enjoying himself so much, I don't complain.

After the beach, he takes me back to the studio. My tummy flutters with nerves, thinking back to Joanna's photo shoot. I've been intimate with Ryan in more ways than I knew were possible before we met, but I'm not sure I want to capture that part of myself on camera. But he doesn't ask me to undress. He gets me a cup of coffee and asks me to stand by one of the tall windows.

The bottom of the windowsill is the perfect height for sitting, and wide enough to almost make a little bench. I sit with one leg up, one foot on the floor, and angle myself so I can look out the window.

"Don't worry about me," Ryan says in that soft, soothing voice he has. "Sip your coffee, look out the window, look at me. Just do whatever feels natural."

I glance out the window and take a sip from the mug, listening to the click of his camera.

"How would you feel about taking your pants off?"

I give him a little smirk. "Suddenly you have to ask?"

"I told you I don't want to make you uncomfortable. I know taking pictures is different. But I think that sweater will just cover your underwear, and that would be sexy as fuck."

I comply, taking off my jeans and tossing them to the side. I sit back in the window, the long sleeves of my sweater pulled over the bottoms of my hands, and the hem reaching just to the top of my thighs. It feels good—flirty and sweet, like I'm being coy. Hiding the good stuff, giving a hint of what's underneath. Ryan takes more pictures, some with me looking away, others with me staring straight at him.

He stops, lowering the camera, and stares at me. "My god, you're beautiful."

I bite my lip and feel my cheeks warm. "Thanks."

He puts his camera on a small table, never taking his eyes off me. I put my coffee down as he stalks across the floor, the intensity in his eyes sending a thrill down my back. He grabs me with strong hands, turning me to face him. Instinctively I wrap my legs around his waist, pulling him close.

Leaning in, he trails kisses down my neck. His hands grab my ass, rubbing me against his hard cock. I tip my head back and moan. He knows exactly how to touch me, exactly how to move. I'm coming alive for him, my body tingling all over. I grab his shirt and he lets go of me long enough to take it off. My hands trail down his shoulders, across his chest, to his deliciously defined abs. Leaning forward, I trace the lines of his shoulder tattoo with my tongue.

Ryan grabs the hem of my sweater and pulls it off. With exquisite slowness, he slides my tank top over my head and unfastens my bra. His hands caress my breasts, teasing my nipples with his thumbs. I moan again.

"How do you do this to me?" He doesn't even have his pants off and I'm already halfway to an orgasm.

He takes my nipple in his mouth, tasting it with his tongue. His mouth works its way up to my collarbone and back down again while I fumble with his jeans. I plunge my hands into his pants as soon as I get them open, gripping his cock. I slide my fingers up and down, squeezing the shaft.

I pull his cock out and move my panties aside.

"Fuck me, Nicole, that's so hot. Put it where you want it."

I tease the tip along the outside, up and down, then rub it against my clit. Fresh waves of pleasure roll through me.

"I love the way you make me feel," I say.

He licks my nipples again and I rub his cock against me, stroking up and down the shaft. His mouth works its way up to my neck, his tongue dancing across my skin.

Without warning, he moves my hand away and grips my hips, hard. He drives his cock into me, pushing me up against the window. I cry out, opening my legs wider for him. He holds me up by my ass, working his cock in and out. His cheek is next to mine, his hot breath against my neck. He fucks me with so much urgency, I claw at his back. He moves faster, harder, so deep it hurts. I gasp, suddenly feeling a jolt of fear.

As if he knows, he stops. He holds still, his cock deep inside me, his chest rising and falling fast against mine. His hands hold my ass so hard it hurts, but his grip slowly releases. He moves his head away just enough to face me, so close our noses almost touch.

His voice is raspy and low. "I love you."

My heart lurches. Oh my god, he said it. The fire in his eyes tells me he's dead serious.

"I love you, too." My voice is breathy, my head spinning. I do love him. More than I've ever loved anyone. Hearing the words spoken aloud feels momentous. I can't believe this is happening.

Ryan pulls out and thrusts in again, gently this time. His eyes don't leave mine. He pushes his cock into me, back and forth, settling into an exquisite rhythm. I rock my hips with his movement, feeling the tension build. My mind is a blur. Nothing exists except the two of us. I am utterly his.

We don't need to say a word, both feeling the first pulses as we climax together. I lean back against the window, my legs wrapped tight around his waist, as ecstasy floods me.

When we both finish, he surrounds me with his arms and holds me close, his face against my neck. I thread my arms around him, enjoying the feel of his skin against mine. We stay there for a long moment, catching our breath.

He pulls away and helps me get my feet on the ground. He watches me as I walk across the studio to his apartment.

I feel so good, but I can't get over the feeling that there is sadness in his eyes.

My heart races, and butterflies seem to have taken up permanent residence in my stomach. Ryan pulls the car into the driveway of a spacious home, right on the beach. It isn't fancy or ostentatious, but I can only imagine what the view must be like from the deck on the roof.

Another car is parked on the street out front. Cody's, perhaps? It sounds like Hunter Evans will be here too. Apparently I'm getting the full Jacobsen family treatment.

My hands tremble with nervousness. What if they don't like me? What if they can see in my eyes what their son and I were doing a few hours ago? I smooth down the folds of my dress. Since Ryan didn't tell me we'd have dinner with his family before I came from Seattle, I only have what I brought with me. Thankfully, I thought to throw a casual lilac dress and a pair of silver sandals in my bag. I showered and blew out my hair, and put on a little makeup before we left, so I feel reasonably put together. But that doesn't seem to be doing anything for the butterflies, which have progressed from fluttering to outright war.

Ryan opens the car door for me. He's been quiet since we had sex that afternoon. Not the sort of quiet that means he might snap at me for something stupid. It's a melancholy sort of quiet. All afternoon, he avoided meeting my eyes, and I had to remind him when we needed to leave. He apologized several times, claiming to be tired, but something seems off. The truth is, something has seemed off for weeks, I just can't pinpoint what it is.

I love you.

The memory of Ryan's words echoes in my mind. I want to bottle that moment—capture it so I can relive it over and over again. He opens the front door and I follow him inside, chewing on my lower lip to keep from smiling too big.

We walk through to the back of the house to find Ryan's family congregated in the spacious kitchen. The conversation dies, and everyone freezes, staring at us with wide eyes.

My smile fades. Why are they staring at me like that?

Ryan puts a reassuring hand on my back. "Hey, everyone. This is Nicole."

Mrs. Jacobsen puts a hand to her chest. Her dark hair is streaked with gray, and she has it swept up in a loose bun. She wears a floral maxi dress and orange cardigan, a chunky necklace at her throat. "Well, for heaven's sake." A smile breaks out across her face and she walks up to me. "Nicole, it is so lovely to meet you. Welcome."

"Thank you so much, Mrs. Jacobsen."

"Please, call me Maureen. Ryan, why didn't you tell us we were finally getting to meet the mysterious Nicole?"

Mysterious? Wait, he didn't... I whip around to look at him. "You didn't tell them I was coming?"

He gives me a sheepish grin. "I wanted it to be a surprise." He turns his grin on his mom and she bats at his arm.

"You're lucky you're cute," she says.

"Sorry, Mom." He moves to give her a big hug.

Cody and Hunter both greet me with hugs, and Ryan's father, Ed, introduces himself and shakes my hand.

"Well," Maureen says, clapping her hands together. "This is wonderful. Hunter, will you take another place setting upstairs for me? Boys, help me bring dinner up to the roof. And someone get a bottle of wine. We need to celebrate."

I follow the family upstairs to the roof. It's absolutely breathtaking. The ocean stretches out as far as the eye can see, sparkling in the evening sun. A large, slatted wood table is set with bright yellow placemats, white plates, and translucent blue glasses. A built-in grill with a stone counter is on one side, and there's comfortable seating everywhere. I played with Ryan as a kid, but I've never actually been to his house. It's beautiful.

Ryan pulls out a chair for me at the table and takes his seat next to mine. The others lay out the food: two platters of pasta with meatballs and marinara sauce, a huge garden salad, and three baskets of French bread. There's so much food, I can't imagine how we'll eat it all. Everyone takes their seats and Ed pours wine.

"So, Nicole," Maureen says, passing a basket of bread. "How long have you been seeing Ryan?"

"Mom," Ryan says. "At least let her eat first."

"What?" Maureen says. "I just want to know."

"Of course you do, Mom," Cody says. He winked at me. "Tell us, Nicole."

"Hey, Cody, how's Jennifer?" Ryan asks.

Cody glares at him. "Really?"

"You drew first blood," Ryan says.

Hunter chuckles and Ed seems to ignore the chatter, focusing on his plate.

"Well," I say. "I guess it's been a few months now?"

"Ah, how nice," Maureen says. She makes a not-so-subtle eyebrow raise at Cody.

Cody smiles and shakes his head, digging into his meal.

The food is delicious. Ryan eats with one hand on my thigh. It's distracting, his touch sending tingles through me. His family makes me feel totally at ease. My nervousness melts away as they talk and laugh. Maureen does a lot of the talking, but she's friendly and sweet. Ryan banters with Cody and Hunter, but I can tell it's good-natured. I feel a little twinge of envy at his relationship with his brothers—because despite the fact that Hunter isn't technically a Jacobsen, the three of them act like brothers. I'm an only child, so I've never had a sibling relationship. His family seems to genuinely enjoy being together, joking and having a good time as they eat.

After dessert, a strawberry rhubarb pie that is to die for, I stand against the railing, looking out over the water. The sun has set, but the moon is out, casting its pale light on the water.

Ryan disappeared downstairs, but he comes back up and settles in next to me at the railing. I shiver in the cool breeze, and he wraps his arms around me.

"This was fun," I say. "Your family is really great."

"Yeah," he says. "They are."

"Do you think they like me?"

"Yes, they like you a lot."

"Are you sure?"

"Absolutely. If my mom didn't like you, she wouldn't have fed you pie."

I laugh, leaning against his warm body.

"Thanks for this. It means a lot to me."

"Of course. It means a lot that you'd bring me here."

He tightens his arms around me, leaning his cheek on my head. His family is amazing, and it seemed like Ryan enjoyed having me here. But there's something else, a feeling I can't put my finger on. Despite the great day, the incredible moments we had, he still seems so sad.

22

RYAN

Nicole needs to get to work early on Monday, so she leaves Sunday afternoon. I can tell she's concerned about me. Despite my assurances that nothing is wrong, her eyes are tight with worry.

Although she offers to stay longer, I more or less push her out the door. I don't want to mess things up at her job. I already feel guilty. For what, I'm not even sure. We had a nice weekend together. My family loved her. She fit right in, talking and laughing like she's been a part of the Jacobsen crew all along. That should lift my spirits, but I spend the rest of the weekend wanting to do nothing more than crawl into bed and stay there.

I made it as far as my couch after Nicole drove away and haven't moved since. I glance up at the clock. Seven-fifteen. I feel groggy, almost as if I've been sleeping, but I know I haven't. My bladder protests, so I muster the energy to get up and use the bathroom.

When I come out, the letter on my dresser catches my eye. It's at the back, a folded sweatshirt covering all but one corner of the white envelope. I put a finger on the edge and slide it out, handling it as if it might burn me.

I've kept that letter for well over a year, unopened. I know who it's from, and I have a good idea of what it says, but I haven't been able to bring myself to read it. Like a fucking idiot, I choose this moment to tear it open.

My eyes scan the words Elise's mother wrote to me. My stomach turns over. Phrases reach out and grab me, hitting me like slaps to the face. *Please don't blame yourself. It wasn't your fault. You did everything you could.*

Meaningless. Words anyone could say. She doesn't know. She wasn't there.

It was my fault. I failed. Elise is dead, and I wasn't strong enough to save her.

I toss the letter to the ground and go back to the couch. Emptiness consumes me. There's a void inside, eating away at everything I am, feeding on any shred of emotion I have left. I don't care. It doesn't matter.

I SPEND the week shuffling between my bed and the couch. When Nicole's car pulls up in the driveway, I don't even know what day it is.

Running a hand through my hair, I get up from the couch. I look down at my shirt and sniff my armpits. Shit, that isn't good. I smell terrible. When did I last shower? Quickly, I snatch up the garbage from the coffee table and shove it under the sink, then dart for the bathroom. Nicole has a key, and I hear her coming in through the studio when I turn on the shower.

The bathroom door handle turns, rattling back and forth. Apparently I locked it.

Nicole's voice comes through the door. "Hey, why did you lock me out?"

I lean my head back, rinsing off the shampoo. "I'll be out in a minute."

She rattles the door handle again. "I could join you."

A spike of irritation shoots through me. I just want a fucking shower. "I said I'll be out in a minute," I say, my voice sharp.

Nicole doesn't answer, and I finish up. I get out and dry off, noticing a glob of toothpaste on the edge of the sink. I probably should have cleaned the bathroom. Knowing Nicole, she won't even mention it—just wipe it up herself and not say anything. There's no reason that thought should make me angry, but it does. She's going to walk through the apartment and put things away, do the things I haven't found the energy to do myself. Then she'll give me that look—her eyebrows drawn together, her lips pressed tight. Pity. She'll look at me with pity, and I don't want to deal with that right now.

Sure enough, she's washing dishes when I come out of the bathroom. I have the towel wrapped around my waist and her eyes rove over me, a little half-smile on her face.

"Hey." She takes a few steps toward me and bites her lower lip.

My dick does nothing. Limp as a fucking noodle. Normally, especially after she's been gone for a week, I'll be hard just at the sight of her. And that little lip nibble? Forget it. But this time, nothing. Son of a bitch, now I can't even get a hard-on. This day just keeps getting better.

I ignore her and go over to my dresser to get some clothes.

"Ryan." Her voice is so soft. She comes up behind me and rubs her hands along my shoulders and down my back. My cock finally stirs. Thank goodness. At least it still works.

I put my hands on the dresser and close my eyes, feeling her hands caress my skin. The hollow space in my chest gapes.

"Are you all right?" she asks.

No. Don't listen to me. I'm lying but I can't bring myself to tell you the truth. "Yeah, I'm fine. I haven't been feeling well this week."

"I'm sorry. Are you sick?"

"Something like that." I grab some cargo shorts and a t-shirt.

"How was your trip?"

"What trip?"

"I thought you were in L.A. this week. Didn't you have a photo shoot?"

Holy shit. I missed it. The art director left me a voicemail, but I haven't bothered to listen to it yet. Fuck. "Right. No, it was canceled."

I slip my feet through a pair of boxer briefs and pull them on.

"Are you sure you want to get dressed right now?"

I pull the shirt over my head.

"Because what I'd like to do is easier without these silly clothes," she says, slipping her hands around my waist.

I step away. My body is responding to her, and for some reason that makes me angry.

"Not now, Nicole."

She stands next to my dresser, gaping at me. I pull on my shorts and go into the kitchen. The apartment suddenly feels so small, like the walls are closing in. There isn't enough room for two people—nowhere for me to get away.

"Is there someone else?" Her voice is so small, so scared.

I look up at her. "No. What are you talking about?"

She tucks her hair behind her ear. "Are you sleeping with someone else?"

"No." How could she even think that? "No, of course not."

"Then what's going on?"

"Nothing."

"But ... I just got here, and I haven't seen you, and you don't want..."

I do want. And I don't. I want the emptiness to go away. I want to feel like I can get out of bed in the morning and work, and take pictures, and fix the front steps, and fuck Nicole until we both scream for mercy. I want to love her like she deserves to be loved. But I can't.

I'm sinking, and I can't take her down with me.

"Not right now. You just got here, and you want me to jump right in and fuck you over the back of the couch?"

Her mouth hangs open and a flash of anger crosses her face. "Why do you keep doing this?"

"Doing what?"

"Being an asshole."

"If I'm such an asshole, why do you keep coming down here every weekend?"

She puts her hands on her hips. "So this is my fault? Seriously, Ryan, there's something wrong with you. One minute you're the most sensitive, generous man I've ever met. Then something changes. You're cold and closed off. Then you apologize and sweet Ryan comes back, and your excuses always sound so damn reasonable."

I stare at the counter and don't answer. She's right. What can I say?

She comes closer. "Talk to me. Tell me what's going on."

I want to. Fuck me, I want to. But this hell I'm living in isn't somewhere I can bear to take her. She's beautiful and sweet and pure. I'll ruin all that. I'll drag her through the mud with me, soiling her along the way. It isn't right. She deserves so much better.

"You know what? This back and forth bullshit, I don't think it's working. We spend all week apart and then you drive down here. It doesn't make any sense. How long are we supposed to keep doing this?"

"I don't know. I guess I thought we'd figure it out."

"Figure what out? There's nothing to figure out. We had some great sex or whatever, but come on, we both knew this couldn't last."

Her lower lip trembles and I look away. I can't bear to see her.

"We had some great sex? That's it? That's all this has been to you?" Her voice rises with every sentence. "What about last weekend? You introduced me to your family."

You asshole. You're hurting her.

But I'll hurt her so much more if she stays.

"Maybe that was a mistake."

I lean against the kitchen counter, my hands pressed against the granite. I don't look up. Without saying a word, Nicole picks up her things and storms out through the studio. Seconds later, the front door slams shut.

I stand there, holding myself up with my arms, feeling like I'll collapse to the floor. Her tires spit gravel as she peels out and zooms up the long driveway.

Just like that, she's gone.

"Fuck!" I throw my head back and yell. I knock over a box of cereal, spilling its contents on the floor, then pick up a mug and launch it at the wall. It smashes, falling to the ground in pieces, and leaves a dent in the drywall.

I run my hands up and down my face. I am such an

asshole. I am the worst fucking human being on the planet. What the hell did I just do to her?

I stumble over to the couch and sit down, leaning my head back. Rain patters against the windows and the waves crash against the sand outside. I close my eyes, feeling the awful void taking over. It's better that she's gone. I never should have gotten involved with her in the first place. I'm not any good for her, and I knew it all along.

She's better off without me.

23

NICOLE

I race down the highway, no idea where I'm even going. Home? I don't really have one. The little room I'm renting is hardly home, and I still haven't found a new apartment. I could go to my parents' house, but I don't want to explain things to my mom. She'll be all practical and remind me how long-distance relationships hardly ever work. The last thing I need is my mother telling me this is for the best.

Trying not to swerve off the road, I send Melissa a quick text. *In town. Need u.*

Tears run down my face. What the hell just happened?

I knew something was wrong as soon as I got to Ryan's house. His apartment was a mess. Dirty clothes were strewn around the floor, to-go cartons sat on the counter, and the sink was full of dishes. I thought I could start things off on the right foot by joining him in the shower, but he wouldn't let me in.

When he came out, wrapped in that towel, little beads of water dripping down his amazing body, I wanted him more than ever. I expected him to come after me, the way he usually does. I even thought about taking my clothes off before he got out of the bathroom, surprising him by sitting naked on his couch, or spreading out on his bed. It's a good thing I didn't. I feel rejected enough as it is; if he'd denied me when I was naked and ready for him, the humiliation would be unbearable.

Not that what he said wasn't bad. The back and forth isn't working? It was a mistake to introduce me to his family?

Sobs choke me, and my shoulders shake. Melissa texts me back. *I'm home. Where are you? Do you need me to come get you?*

I tap a reply. *On my way.*

My vision blurs and the rain pelts down. I hurt so bad, I want to throw up. Or scream. Or punch someone. Maybe all of the above. Why is Ryan doing this?

Why did I let myself fall so hard for him?

I make it into town without crashing and pull up in front of Melissa's little house. Moss-green with white trim, her house has daffodils growing out front and a gravel path leading to the door. I hop out and dash through the rain. Not that I care about getting wet. I must look a mess, as hard as I've been crying.

Melissa throws open the door before I even have a chance to knock. "What happened? No, don't talk yet."

She ushers me to the couch and wraps a fluffy blanket around my shoulders. I take shaky breaths and try to stop crying, but the tears keep coming. Clutching at the blanket, I settle into the cushions and wait while she bustles around the kitchen.

Melissa emerges with a serving tray bearing a mug of steaming tea, two shot glasses filled with amber liquid, and a bowl of potato chips.

"I don't have any ice cream," she says and puts the tray down on the coffee table.

I sniff. "That's okay."

She hands me the shot and takes the other one for herself. I toss it back. Tequila. It goes down easily, spreading warmth through my belly.

"There's more where that came from. Now, spill."

I wipe the back of my hand beneath both eyes. "I think Ryan just broke up with me."

"He did what?" she asks, her eyes wide. "Oh, hell no." She snatches her phone off the table.

"What are you doing?"

"I'm texting Ryan to tell him what a dumbfuck he is."

"No, Mel, don't," I say, my voice pleading.

She groans, but tosses her phone down next to her. "Fine. I'll wait. Tell me what happened."

"I don't even know. Honestly, things have been up and down for a while. Mostly up, but he gets in these moods. It's like he's tired and doesn't want to do anything. I've been worried about him, but he always claims he's fine."

"He's a guy. They always say they're fine."

"Yeah. So, I showed up this morning and from the minute I walked in, he was acting weird. Like he wasn't even happy to see me. He came out of the shower, and normally we'd start off with some mind-blowing sex, but he said no. There he is, dressed in nothing but a towel, and I was practically throwing myself at him."

"He turned down sex?"

"Yep. Totally shot me down."

"Shit."

"Right? I was so shocked, I didn't know what to say. My first thought was he'd been sleeping with someone else. He was so cold and distant." My voice breaks, and I take another breath to steady myself. "When Jason was cheating on me, that's how he acted. He avoided me, wouldn't look at me."

"Do you think Ryan is cheating?"

"No. I asked, straight up, and he said no. I believe him. There wasn't any dishonesty in his voice when he denied it. And unless the girl is a slob, he hasn't had anyone else in his apartment in a while."

"Good, because if he was cheating on you, I'd have to do more than text him. Dick-punch the fucker, maybe."

I shake my head. "No, but it doesn't matter. He said this isn't working. Then he said introducing me to his family last week was a mistake."

"He really said that?"

"Yeah." I pull the blanket around my shoulders. I want to disappear inside it. "Last weekend he told me he loved me." My voice trembles and fresh tears run down my face. "He said it, Mel. Why did he say that if he didn't mean it?"

Melissa puts her arm around my shoulder and draws me in. "Oh, sweetie."

I rest my head on her shoulder, crying softly. I feel like I was run over. Everything hurts.

"I'm so sorry this happened." She rubs slow circles around my back. "You'll be okay. We'll get you through this."

24

NICOLE

When I caught Jason cheating, I felt like my life was at an end. Everything stopped. I fell apart. I cried in front of Sandra, ran away to my parents' house, and spent my days feeling sorry for myself. Looking back, I hate the way I acted. Being upset is normal. I spent a lot of time believing my life was going in a certain direction, and in one second, it all came undone. But what really bothered me, what I mourned more than the loss of Jason, was the loss of the story I created.

I wanted to impress people, to show them a small-town girl could go out and live the dream. For a while, I thought I was. Popular boyfriend, college degree, great job, surely that marriage proposal right around the corner.

But none of it was real. The boyfriend was anything but great. My job might sound important, but it's boring. The marriage proposal? Well, thank goodness he never did, because what a disaster that would have been. I held onto that life for years longer than I should have—I can see that now. I did what I thought was expected of me, tried to hold the threads of that fairy tale together. Wasn't that what I was supposed to do? Isn't life a set of steps, one leading to the next, moving you on to the next, better thing?

No. It really isn't.

So I let myself wallow in misery after Jason. I'm not going to let myself get away with that again.

Ryan has hurt me far more than Jason ever did. It's easy to look back and realize Jason and I were never good for each other. As teenagers, maybe, but even then it was more like we dated each other because the choices were limited.

But Ryan... He got inside my soul. I felt connected to him in ways I never dreamed could be real. It was like something in a movie. He set my blood on fire. He made me feel special, taken care of, loved.

He made me feel brave.

Despite how much the loss of him hurts, I go back to Seattle determined not to crumble. I can cry myself to sleep every night, in the privacy of my room, but I will not let this derail my entire life. I go to work and do my job. I make phone calls and update my spreadsheets and order programs for the next event.

Working on the art festival is harder, but I do it. I answer emails, tick off my to-do list, check in with people to make sure everything is ready. I receive a very surprising phone call from the mayor, who tells me she's looking forward to the event, and she's heard from numerous people in town that I'm doing a great job.

I even hear from Jackson Bennett. I completely forgot about my email to him, then his name pops up in my inbox. It's brief, but says he'll be at the festival, and to let him know when and where to find me so we can talk about details. I'm not sure what he means, but I answer, telling him I can meet him at the gallery at nine in the morning on the first day of the event.

On a Tuesday afternoon, my office is quiet. I glance through my emails, feeling sleepy with boredom, while I print off a set of thank-you letters. Sandra appears next to my desk. Her dark hair is pulled back, the front teased up, and her lips are painted bright red. She wears a pinstripe jacket and pencil skirt, a white blouse underneath, and shiny black pumps. She always makes me feel underdressed, although no one else in the office dresses as formally as she does.

"Did you make sure the table cards went to the printer for next week?" she asks.

"Yes, that's all taken care of."

"And the guest list?"

"It's on the server and I left a printed copy on your desk."

"Right. Thanks."

She walks back to her office. I sigh, sitting back in my chair, and think about all the menial tasks she still gives me. Why did she promote me to Events Manager if all she needs me to do is busywork? Anyone can print guest lists and order table cards. I expected she would have me actually *managing* the events, but I'm still nothing but her little lackey. She even has an actual assistant, but I'm surprised she doesn't ask me to get her morning coffee.

This is ridiculous. I'm perfectly capable of handling more responsibility. I'm single-handedly running a community art festival, and I'm doing that in my spare time while living three hours away.

I get up and go to Sandra's office. The door is open, but I knock.

"Can I talk to you for a second?"

She waves me in and I take the seat across her desk. Her eyes stay on her screen and her fingers tap her keyboard.

"What's up, Nicole?" she asks.

"I've been thinking. You promoted me to Events Manager over a year ago, but I feel like my job hasn't really changed very much. I'd really like to take on some additional responsibility."

She stops typing and looks at me. "You're doing a great job. You don't have anything to worry about."

"No, I'm not worried. And I appreciate that you think I'm doing a great job. But I can do a lot more than you're currently having me do."

"What do you suggest?"

"Well," I say, gathering my courage, "the silent auction for the Myer Foundation is coming up this fall. It isn't a large event, and I helped with it last year. I'd like to take it on, make it mine. I know I'm ready for this."

Sandra takes a deep breath. "I don't know if that's necessary, Nicole. The Myer auction is a lot of work. I know it seems like it's small, but there are a lot of details."

"I'm great at details. You know that."

"You're right, you are. But Lisa always runs the Myer auction. I can't just take it from her."

"Okay, then what about something else? All I do all day is print thank you letters and call a few vendors."

"Nicole, your job is important."

Is it? I pause. "Why did you promote me to Events Manager if you didn't plan to change my responsibilities?"

Did I just say that out loud?

Sandra purses her lips, making little red lines stand out along the edges. "Nicole, you're good at what you do. You're personable and organized. I appreciate that. I gave you that title to keep you happy. It seemed like it would mean a lot to you to have it on your business card, but I wasn't planning on actually changing your job. I need you doing what you're doing. If you want me to call you Events Manager, I don't have a problem with that. But your job is what it is. If things change, or someone else moves on, I'll certainly consider you for their role. Until then, just keep doing what you're doing. Someday, when you're ready to move on, this will look great on your resume."

I look down at my hands in my lap. This is what I wanted, isn't it? The title? The image? I can tell people I'm an Events Manager, brag about how we organize conferences and luncheons for software companies and big non-profits. It does look good. It makes me look successful, and isn't that exactly what I was after?

The answer is so simple, I'm amazed it took me this long to figure it out.

"Sandra, I want to thank you so much for this opportunity. You've been very nice, and I'll always appreciate how understanding you were when I was going through some personal stuff. But this will be my two-week notice."

Sandra stares at me, her bright red lips open. "You're quitting?"

"I'm sorry to spring this on you, but I haven't been happy here for a long time. I stayed at this job for all the wrong reasons, and I'm just not willing to do that to myself anymore."

She watches me get up, but doesn't say anything as I walk out of her office. I go back to my desk, feeling suddenly lighter. There's no doubt in my mind this is the right decision. I have no idea what I'm going to do in two weeks—what I'll do for work, or where I'll live. From the outside, my life looks like an absolute fucking disaster.

What is my mother going to say?

But I honestly don't care. For the first time in my life, I ignore the voice in my head, warning me of what everyone else is going to say about me. I need to make a change for me, not for them, and if other people don't like it, they can whisper whatever they want. The truth is, no one is scrutinizing my life that way, and I need to stop living like they are.

I don't have Ryan, and the pain of it is an acute ache that won't go away. I miss him terribly. But I'll pick up the pieces and forge ahead, making my own way. Ryan broke my heart into a thousand pieces, but he showed me I can be strong. I can be brave. I can take risks and do things I've been afraid to try.

I'll have to thank him for that someday.

25

RYAN

It occurs to me someone has been knocking at the door. Pounding on it, as a matter of fact. I set my XBOX controller down and look around, bewildered. What time is it? Six-thirty. Is that a.m. or p.m.? Shit, I honestly have no idea. Judging by the light, it's evening. That makes sense. I didn't sleep much last night, and I've more or less stayed on the couch playing *Halo* all day.

Someone bangs on the door again. I get up, glancing at my phone on my way into the studio. A dozen missed calls and just as many texts. Crap, I left it on silent. None of them are from Nicole. *Fuck.* Of course not. I made sure of that.

Still. Fuck.

"Ryan!" Cody's voice through the door.

"Yeah, yeah, I'm coming."

I open the door to find Cody, with Hunter standing just behind him.

"Oh my god, Ryan," Cody says. "You scared the fuck out of everyone."

I step aside and let them in. "Why? I've been here all day. I'm fine."

Cody's brow draws down and he gives me a look that rivals our mom's interrogation face. "Are you?"

No. I'm drowning and I don't care enough to even try to breathe. "Yeah. I just needed to chill. It's nothing."

Cody and Hunter share a look while I shut the door. I don't think they believe me.

"Then why weren't you answering your phone?" Cody asks.

I hold it up. "I had it switched to silent. Sorry, man. I haven't been sleeping well, so I didn't want some alert to wake me up. I forgot to turn the ringer back on."

Cody casts his eyes up at the ceiling, shaking his head. "Son of a bitch, Ryan. You can't do that. We were worried. Mom's been freaking out."

"Hey, I said I was sorry. Calm down. You guys want a beer or something?"

"I could definitely use a beer," Hunter says.

Cody nods. "After the last couple of hours, I need more than a beer. Let me call mom first. Then I say we make a bonfire on the beach and get shit-faced."

"I'm in," Hunter says.

I don't particularly want to do anything other than sit on my couch and maybe play some more *Halo*. But I have a feeling Cody and Hunter are going to stay no matter what, so I grunt something noncommittal and shuffle into my apartment to grab a sweatshirt and the beer.

"What the hell, Ryan?" Hunter asks from the doorway to my apartment.

"What?"

"Are you on an all-chip diet now?" he asks with a laugh.

I glance at my couch. Discarded bags and wrappers are strewn all over the couch, floor, and coffee table. I left beer bottles and soda cans lying wherever I put them down. It seemed like too much work to clean up.

"Yeah, sorry." I try to think of a decent excuse for the mess, but come up with nothing, so I just shrug.

Cody gives me the side-eye again, but doesn't say anything. I grab a six-pack out of the fridge and hand it to Hunter while Cody gets a bottle of Jack Daniels out of the cupboard.

"Getting serious," Hunter says, nodding toward the bottle of Jack.

"It's been that kind of day," Cody says.

We take our drinks and a few plastic cups down to the beach, along with three camping chairs. Cody, my dad, and I made a fire ring at the base of the dunes, far enough up the beach that even the highest tides don't reach it. Cody and I gather some small pieces of driftwood and Hunter gets the fire going. We set our chairs in a ring around the fire, and drink our beers in silence while the flames crackle.

When I'm on my second beer, the Jack still sitting next to my chair, Cody breaks the silence. "So, Hunter found a house to rent in town."

I'm so relieved he didn't ask about me, engaging in conversation doesn't seem so terrible. "Nice. Where?"

"Close to downtown," Hunter says. "It's small, but I don't need much space."

"I guess that means you're staying."

"Yeah, I told you, I'm here. You guys are stuck with me." He lifts up his beer and takes a swig.

Cody and I drink to that. I have to admit, it's good to have Hunter home. It feels a bit like old times, the three of us together.

"Have you seen Emma yet?" Cody asks.

Hunter winces. "No."

Emma was Hunter's girlfriend before he left. She was as shocked and devastated by his sudden departure as anyone.

"You should go see her," Cody says. "It's been a long time. I bet she'd be happy to see you."

"I doubt that," Hunter says. "Plus, she's not exactly single anymore."

"Ouch," Cody says. "Sorry, I hadn't heard that."

"Yeah," Hunter says. "I still need to go see her. I owe her an apology at least."

"What about you, Ryan?" Cody asks. "How's Nicole?"

I shift in my chair, my eyes locked on the fire. "I don't know."

"Is she in Seattle?" Cody asks.

"Yeah."

Cody finishes off his beer and sets the bottle in the sand. "What's going on?"

"I'm having beers on the beach with you guys."

Cody goes silent for a while, and I hope he stays that way. The sky darkens as the sun goes down, and a light breeze blows the smoke out across the dunes.

"Does she know?" Cody asks.

"Does she know what?" I ask, although I know what he means.

"Don't pretend to be an idiot," Cody says.

I don't look up. "No." I gesture with my beer bottle toward Hunter. "Does he know?"

"Yeah. I told him on the way up here."

"Man, if I'd known..." Hunter says, trailing off. "I'm an asshole. I didn't know what was going on, and that's my fault for being a dick and staying away. I should have been here. I'm sorry."

I shake my head. "It wasn't your fault."

"Do you remember when your therapist had us all come in?" Cody asks. "Dad, Mom, and I all met with him."

"Sure, I remember."

"He told us what to watch out for," Cody says. "He said there would be signs that things were going bad again, that you were backsliding. Fuck if I haven't been seeing every one of them lately. You're withdrawn. You don't answer calls. When I do see you, I can't tell if you're listless or simply tired. You cancel plans. I'm not going to sit by and let this happen."

I don't know what to say. He's right. I've slipped so far down, so fast, but I can't make myself care. "There's nothing for you to do. I'm kind of down, but it's no big deal. I just need to deal with it on my own."

"You should tell Nicole," Cody says.

"Why?" I ask, looking up. "So she can know what a fucking mess I am? Besides, we broke up."

"You what?" Cody asks. "You did not. What the fuck happened?"

I am not going to rehash the details. "It wasn't working out."

"Ryan, you dumbass," Cody says. "Don't you see what's happening? This isn't you. This is the depression again. She needs to know. You still care about her, don't you?"

I grab the bottle of Jack, open it, and pour some into each of the three cups. Cody and Hunter both take theirs. Plastic cups might not be the classiest way to drink whiskey, but it works on the beach. I toss it back, feeling the heat trail down my throat and spread through my gut.

"Yes, I care about her." I push my cup down into the sand so it won't blow over. "Maybe too much. That's part of the problem."

"Why is that a problem?" Cody asks. "I hadn't seen you

happy like that since I don't even know when. What was so wrong with that?"

"She deserves better. This is my life. I feel good for a while, but then this happens. The thing with Elise, that wasn't even the first time. It was just the worst. I'm fucked up and broken and Nicole should have someone whole."

"Maybe that should be her call," Cody says.

I hunker down in my chair, refusing to answer.

"You know, sometimes a person comes into your life who's worth fighting for," Hunter says. "Even if that fight is with yourself."

I pinch the bridge of my nose and shake my head. I want to lash out at Hunter, but I stop myself. I'm angry because he's right.

"Okay, man. You'll figure it out," Cody says. He holds out his cup. "In the meantime, answer your fucking phone when we call, and pour me some more whiskey."

I WAKE the next morning hungover as shit. Cody and Hunter are sprawled out, Cody on the couch and Hunter sideways in an armchair. I hardly remember getting back to my house last night. After polishing off the bottle of Jack, we staggered up the beach and collapsed.

I roll out of bed and head straight for the shower. I'm pretty sure I managed to get sand in my ass crack. I have faint memories of wrestling Hunter to the ground. Probably not the best idea, but whiskey tends to do that.

Cody and Hunter are still asleep when I get out of the shower, so I dress quietly to let them sleep. I grab a clean shirt and pull a pocket-sized spiral notebook out of my nightstand drawer. I haven't looked at that battered little notebook in months, but I know it's time to face what's happening to me. Cody is right. The signs are there. I have the tools to get better, I just need to pick myself up off my couch and start using them.

Suddenly, that idea feels insurmountable. This stupid notebook can't fix me. What's the point?

I think about Nicole and push the thought away. I love her. Fuck me, I love her so much it cuts through the deadness. It makes me feel something, even if it's mostly a shit load of guilt for being such an asshole. I absolutely hate myself for what I did to her, but Hunter was right. She's worth fighting for.

But I can't go back to her like this. I'm right, too—she does deserve better. I don't know if I can give it to her, and the thought is almost too much. But I'll never be able to live with myself if I don't try.

I walk outside and down to the beach. Our chairs are still around the fire pit, although the fire is nothing but a pile of blackened coals. I sit down and cross an ankle over one knee, and open the notebook.

It's a list my therapist and I made. An emergency plan, so to speak. Each page has a single item, so none of them seem too overwhelming. When I feel myself slipping, I'm supposed to follow the notebook. I should have started months ago, when I first started feeling down, but ignoring the problem is a lot easier than facing it. Now it's time to start clawing my way out of this pit before I find the bottom.

I already know what the first page says: *Twenty minutes of sunlight every day.* The breeze is chilly, but the sky is clear, so I take off my shirt and stretch out my legs. I close my eyes and soak in the sun, feeling the rays warm my skin.

I know what the second page says, too: *Go to the gym.* I have the list memorized, but the words on the page, written in my own handwriting, help center me. When did I last go to the gym? Weeks ago? No wonder I feel like shit. It isn't just last night's whiskey.

After sitting in the sun for a while, I go back inside. I know it would be a mistake to power through the whole list in one day. If I try to do too much too soon, I'll burn out fast and feel like a failure. Then I'll be worse off than before I started. But going to the gym sounds really good. I want to feel my body move, lift, stretch. I'll work out, eat, and call it a day—leave the rest of the list for later. I can do that. I can get through today.

Every day after, I work the list. I tell Cody to call me at night and ask me what I did to feel better, and apologize in advance for when I'll be a dick about it. But I need the accountability. I start each day with a walk on the beach, even when I don't feel like getting up. I go to the gym. I'm so sore for the first few days, I almost quit going, but Hunter comes over and drags me in with him. I have dinner at my mom's every night for a week, clearing my system of all the shit I've been eating. I start taking my vitamins again. I hang out with my brothers, go out for a beer with my dad. I even text Cody and Hunter when I'm having a particularly bad night. They come over and play XBOX. Just having them there keeps me from sinking too far.

Mostly, I think about Nicole.

It takes me a while before I get up the courage to process the photos I took of her. Seeing her on my computer screen, breathtakingly beautiful, makes my chest tight. I want so badly to call her, to tell her I'm doing better, but I know I'm not ready. Months of backsliding into depression won't go away overnight, and I can't drag her into this too soon. I'll only hurt her again.

If I have any chance at getting her back, I need to be

prepared to be honest with her. To be real. To stop hiding the worst parts of me and let her see them. It's scary as fuck, but I know it's the only way. If she can't handle it, I'll have to deal with the consequences, and I'm more than a little convinced she can't. There's a lot I've kept from her.

I'm not sure how to approach her when the time comes. I haven't tried to contact her since the Great Asshole Episode, and I have no idea if she'll even answer my call. This isn't something I can tell her over the phone, anyway. I need to see her in person. I could drive up to Seattle and surprise her, but I realize I don't have the address of where she's living. I know where she works, so I could probably find her there, but that seems like it could backfire pretty spectacularly.

She'll be in town for the art festival, but she'll be busy. I'm not sure how to get her alone. Unless I have help.

I grab my phone and take a deep breath. This is a big risk. There's no way I'm not on the outs with the best friend. And Melissa kind of scares me.

I type out a text, deciding to go for it and be as honest as possible.

Hey. It's Ryan the Asshole. I know you hate me. I deserve it. But I love her. I screwed up—a lot. Please help me get her back.

I wait, my gut churning with nervousness. My phone lights up with a reply.

Are you fucking serious?

I blow out another breath.

Dead fucking serious. I love her like crazy. I'll do anything.

Minutes pass with no reply. Is she calling Nicole to tell her what a jackass I am? Did I make the right decision to contact Melissa?

Okay. If you really love her, I'm in. But if you screw this up again I'll punch you in the dick.

I lean back against the couch cushions, relief washing over me. I do love her. I love her with everything I am. I'm terrified it's too late and I've already lost her. But I can't give up. I'll be honest, and bare my soul, letting her see the demons inside. I just hope she loves me enough to forgive me, and accept me for the mess of a man that I am.

26

NICOLE

*J*etty Beach is pretty much the last place I want to be. It's impossible to go anywhere without running into reminders of Ryan. I have thoughts of taking off, driving across country, with no plan or destination in mind. I don't have a job or an apartment tying me down, so why not? Why do I have to shuffle back to the beach with my tail between my legs ... again?

But the truth is, I'm not back with my tail between my legs. Sure, things are uncertain and I have no idea what I'm going to do next, but there's freedom in that. I have a little money saved, so I'll be okay for a few months while I figure out what to do. And I still have a festival to pull off. If I do nothing else this summer, I am going to throw the best damn art festival Jetty Beach has ever seen.

Melissa insisted I come stay with her, although her place is tiny. I don't mind. I can sleep on the couch, and the thought of living with my parents again threatens to ruin what bit of good mood I'm still capable of. Mel chats with me like usual, but doesn't ask too many questions. We talk about how things had ended at my job. I did my two weeks and handed off my responsibilities to others. Sandra assured me she would give me a glowing recommendation when the time came, and wished me well.

I'm grateful Melissa doesn't talk about Ryan, although I wonder if she's seen him around town. It's likely. Jetty Beach isn't the sort of place people can disappear. Of course, he might still be holed up in his house. Who knows how often he goes out? I haven't heard a word from him since the day I left. The pain of missing him hasn't diminished. I'm proud of myself for living through it, for not falling to pieces. But I still cry at night, when I'm sure Melissa won't hear.

There's definitely something Melissa isn't telling me though. On the second night I was here, I noticed her texting back and forth with someone, angling the screen so I couldn't see. Little smiles crossed her lips, and once she stopped herself from laughing out loud. I wondered if she'd met someone, and was surprised she wouldn't tell me—but figured maybe she wasn't ready to talk about it. I could understand that.

I don't ask questions, but I hope he's someone great. One of us deserves to be happy.

With the festival so close, I have plenty to do. I settle into a routine, working on the festival during the day, hanging out with Melissa at night. She's finishing up her school year, busy working on report cards. I start going for runs on the beach—I'm afraid to join the local gym because I know Ryan works out there. I see Cody's car in the grocery store parking lot once and decide to drive around until he leaves. Maybe that's childish, but I don't know what to say to him. But as often as I'm out and about in town, I never run into Ryan.

I wake up early on a Wednesday morning. Melissa is

already hunched over her coffee at the little table in the kitchen, and I pour myself a cup. The festival is starting in just two days, and I have a lot of work to do.

"Hey," she says, looking up from her paperwork.

"How's it going this morning?"

"Oh, you know me and my glamorous life," she says with a smile. "It's going fine, actually. I'm almost done. But teacher burnout in June is a real thing."

"I bet."

"Are you going out this morning?"

"Yeah, I need to get down to the gallery and start moving some things around for Friday."

She taps her pen against her lips. "Would you do me a favor?"

"Sure."

"I have to be at work in like half an hour, but I'm expecting a package today, and it needs a signature. The tracking email says it's scheduled for delivery by ten. Can you stay here until then and sign for it?"

I take a sip of my coffee. I want to get started earlier, but it shouldn't matter. Melissa is nice enough to put me up; I can certainly help her out. "Yeah, I'll stay. You're sure it's coming this morning?"

"Positive."

"What is it?"

She stands and gathers up her papers. "Oh, you know, just something I ordered. I don't know why they won't leave it on the porch. But if someone's not here to get it, they'll hold it at the post office, and then I have to go down there to pick it up. And we both know how much fun Agnes is."

Agnes has been running the post office since we were kids. She isn't exactly friendly.

"Yeah, that's no fun. Don't worry about it. I'll be here."

"Thanks, Nic."

I pass the time reading a book on the couch with another cup of coffee. Melissa is at work, and her house is blissfully quiet. Although I intended to get an earlier start on the day, it's nice to sit by myself and forget my troubles for a while.

The knock at the door startles me, even though I know to expect it. I set down my mug, put my book aside, and get up to answer the door.

My heart literally jumps and my stomach does a somersault when I see who it is. Ryan.

"Please don't slam the door," he says, putting a hand on the door to keep it open.

I can't move. I just stare at him. He looks good. The dark circles are gone from under his eyes and his jaw is back to the neatly trimmed stubble I love so much. I can just make out the lines of his chest and abs beneath his shirt and his eyes are intense, green and smoldering.

"Nicole, may I please talk to you?"

His voice is so sweet. I'm torn between wanting to hit him across the face for hurting me, and throwing my arms around his neck and holding him.

"Yeah, I guess so."

I step aside and let him in. My heart won't stop racing. He glances around, as if he isn't sure what to do.

"Should we sit down?"

I sink onto the couch, scooting the blanket and my book out of the way. Ryan sits next to me, close enough I could touch him, but not so near as to intrude on my personal space. He sits looking straight ahead and runs his hands up and down his thighs.

"I owe you an apology," he says. "I owe you a lot more

than that, but first I want you to know how sorry I am. For everything. I hurt you in so many ways and I hate myself for it. I was going through something and I tried to keep it from you. I know that's no excuse for how I acted, and especially not for the things I said. But I am so sorry."

He pauses, licking his lips, and looks down as if gathering his thoughts. I pull the edges of the blanket closer.

"I have something I need to tell you, and this isn't easy for me. I know this is going to seem out of place, but I need to tell you about Elise."

I nod. Elise? His ex-girlfriend? Where is this going?

"I met Elise on a shoot in L.A. She was a model. At first we were just friends. Truth be told, I felt bad for her and thought she could use someone to talk to. It seemed like she had a lot of drama in her life. There was never a point when we decided we were together. It just sort of happened. Pretty soon she was crashing at my place so often, she basically lived there. I found out later she'd been evicted from her apartment, but she was pretty good at hiding things from me."

I listen quietly, not sure what to say.

"In any case, Elise had problems. After we'd been together for about a year, she confessed to using prescription pain killers. A lot. I was pissed. I'd been driving her to doctor's appointments, believing her story that she had some sort of autoimmune disease and the doctors were all idiots who didn't know how to help her. The truth was, she would come up with a story for every new doctor, until they would quit prescribing for her. Then she'd move on to another one. When she told me, I was ready to ask her to leave. Our relationship was a disaster. But she told me about her addiction, and asked for my help.

"What was I supposed to say to that? I felt like I couldn't leave her. Her family was out in Ohio and she didn't have any other friends. Not real friends anyway. So I put all my energy into helping her. She refused to go to rehab, but I thought I could do it. I nursed her through withdrawal. I drove her to meetings and sat in the back while people talked about their addictions. I canceled shoots so I didn't have to travel. I even tried to convince her to move up here. I didn't think L.A. was the best place for her to make a good recovery. She was still surrounded by all the same pressures. Still, after a while, she got better. She started working again. Her career really took off. She got some high profile gigs. It was good."

"Until?" I ask, my voice quiet.

"Until it wasn't, I guess. Our relationship wasn't any better, even with her sober. Later, I spent way too much time trying to get my therapist to help me analyze what went wrong, but the truth was, I didn't love her. I liked her. I wanted her to be happy. But I didn't want to be with her. I don't know if she sensed that and it contributed to her relapse, or what. But she did relapse. Hard. I should have seen it coming, but it took me by surprise. I found a discarded pill bottle next to the dumpster outside our apartment building. She'd been throwing the bottles away outside so I wouldn't see them, but she'd dropped one. I confronted her and she broke down, sobbing. She'd been using again for weeks. So I got back to work. I took her to a meeting. I fed her soup. I rented light-hearted movies to get her mind off things. I thought it was just a bump in the road, and I could get her through it. Unfortunately, I was wrong."

Ryan takes a shaking breath. I want to reach out and put my hands on his. He looks down at the floor and keeps talking.

"I'd been sleeping on the couch for a long time by then. We'd never talked about it; I just quit sleeping in the bedroom. I got up one morning and made her breakfast. It was a Monday. I was supposed to have a shoot that day, but it wasn't until three, so I figured I could take my time. By noon, she hadn't come out, so I went in to check on her."

I gasp and put my hands to my mouth. I know what he's going to say.

"I could tell she was dead as soon as I opened the door. One arm was falling off the bed at a weird angle and her skin looked blue. Half a bottle of Vicodin and another bottle without a label were on the nightstand. The authorities determined it probably wasn't on purpose. She left a lot of pills sitting there. If she meant to commit suicide, she would have taken more. Her body just couldn't take it. She took those pills one time too many, and it killed her."

"Oh, Ryan," I say through my fingers.

"That's not even the worst of it. I had to tell you about Elise so you'll understand what happened next."

He pauses, covering his mouth with his hand. He takes another deep breath.

"I told her family, of course, but I didn't really talk about it to anyone else. I kept to myself those years I lived in L.A., and my parents hadn't even met her. It was the weirdest thing. Whether I'd been in love with her or not, she'd been a part of my life for two years. I found her body in my bed. But I didn't feel anything. I wasn't mad, I wasn't upset. I was numb. I started to wonder if there was something wrong with me. I took a tearful phone call from her sister, and I felt nothing. I helped arrange to have her remains sent to her family, and it was no different from going to the post office."

"After a while, I quit doing things," he says. "It happened so gradually, I almost didn't notice. I cancelled shoots, turned down jobs. I didn't go out much. I stopped calling home, didn't answer my phone. I sat around a lot. I started to feel like maybe I died when Elise did, only my body hadn't caught on yet. I felt like a ghost, just drifting through the world. I didn't care. I should have known something was wrong when I was supposed to go to the Caribbean for a shoot, and I just didn't go. I got up that day, knew I had a flight to catch, sat down on the couch, and didn't move. Later, when a therapist told me it was clinical depression it made a lot of sense. But at the time, I thought I would just fade into nothingness. And maybe the world would be better off."

I clutch the blanket to my chest. My heart feels like bursting.

"It got a lot worse. I didn't eat much. I went days without leaving my apartment. I should have moved, but even that seemed like too much work. I lost out on jobs because I kept flaking out, but I couldn't make myself care. I was so numb, I thought I was becoming a monster. I started having a lot of obsessive thoughts." He pauses again and when he continues, his voice is quiet. "I don't want to tell you the rest."

I drop the blanket and reach out, putting a hand on top of his. "It's okay. You can tell me."

"I felt like, if I was a corpse walking around, I might as well stop pretending. Like an idiot, I'd kept a bunch of Elise's pills. So I swallowed them and went to bed, fully intending not to wake up."

Tears spring to my eyes and my stomach turns over. "Oh god, Ryan. What happened then? How did you..."

"How did I not die? Cody. I texted him right before I took the pills. Honestly, I don't remember what I said, but it scared him enough that he called the police and convinced them to break in. They busted down the door and rushed me to the hospital."

I stare at him, my hand still over his. I want to wrap him in my arms and never let him go, but I can tell he isn't finished.

"When I got out of the hospital, my parents drove all the way down and picked me up. They brought me back here, let me crash at their place, took me to therapy. I started to get better, and I decided to stay. This place is good for me. I bought the church and started restoring it. The work helped a lot. I had purpose again, and day by day, I found it got easier. By the time I met you, I was in a good place. I was healthy."

I shift in my seat and he puts his other hand over mine, but he doesn't turn to look at me.

"My therapist told me I could expect to relapse. He gave me tools to cope if I did, made sure I understood what to look out for. He told my family the same thing. But when it started a few months ago, I tried to ignore it. What did I have to be depressed about? I had you. I should have been happy. That just made it worse. I was angry at myself for not being normal, for not being able to enjoy the best thing that ever happened to me. I took that out on you. I tried to push you away because I was afraid. I thought I'd only hurt you if you stayed with me. I was too broken."

"You should have told me. I would have helped you."

"I know. I should have trusted you enough to tell you everything. That's why I'm here now. I screwed up. I don't know if I can ever make it up to you, but I'm willing to try."

He squeezes my hand and slowly turns to look at me, his green eyes locking with mine. "Even though I've been the biggest asshole imaginable, what got me through this was you. I love you, Nicole. I've loved you since the first time I touched you. I was afraid of it. I thought it was too good for me, that I'd taint it somehow. But it's so much bigger than me."

My body trembles. Ryan brushes my hair back from my face and leans closer.

"I can't promise you that I'll never have a hard time again. But I can promise that I won't keep it from you. I'll ask for help when I need it. Please, Nicole, please forgive me."

A tear breaks free from the corner of my eye. "Of course I forgive you."

Ryan smiles—that gorgeous, irresistible smile. "I love you."

"I love you too."

He presses his lips against mine and my eyes flutter closed. I breathe deep, taking in his scent. His arms wrap around me, and my body lights up. Our kiss goes from gentle to passionate. His tongue glides into my mouth and he grabs my hips, pulling me onto his lap.

"I missed you so much." He kisses me again before I can answer, his mouth hungry for mine.

I slide my hands down to his cock and grip it through his pants. He groans and nibbles on my lower lip.

I need him so badly I can barely stand it. I unfasten his pants and he pulls off my shirt.

"Are you sure we should do this here?" he asks, breathing hard.

I pause, glancing around. "She's at work and I don't care."

He grins, pushing me back onto the couch. He frees his cock while I pull off my pants. There is no waiting, no teasing. I ache for him and he plunges inside me, my hands on his ass, grinding him deeper.

"Oh my god, Nicole," he says, speaking softly into my ear. "I don't want to be without you ever again."

The feel of him inside me is bliss. He makes me feel whole. I want to be his, to have all of him, broken parts and all.

"You never have to be."

EPILOGUE: NICOLE

I wait for Jackson Bennett at the art gallery, half-convinced he won't show up. I don't have much time. It's nine o'clock, and the festival is set to kick off at ten. I need most of that hour to run around and make sure everything is in place. Of course, Ryan is doing some of that running around for me. He put up the new banners, made sure the food trucks set up in the right places, and wandered through the line of canopies, making sure the artists have everything they need.

I don't know how I would have done it without him.

Melissa confessed to setting me up, making sure I'd be there when Ryan came over. I told her I got her back by letting him fuck me senseless on her couch. She said she'd send me the cleaning bill.

I wander around the gallery, waiting. I've done what I can to help make the place more inviting. The current owners are pretty hands-off, and the person they've hired to run things didn't mind me moving things around. I tried to organize the art so there's some order, grouping displays by artist or by medium. I put my hands on my hips and look around. It isn't half-bad. It still needs some hard-core renovations, but for this event, it will do.

The door opens and Jackson Bennett walks in. He's in a cream-colored button-down shirt and a pair of brown slacks. His look is understated, but he still drips *expensive* from head to toe.

"Hi," I say.

"Hi." He pauses for a second. "Nicole."

"Yes." I hold out my hand and he shakes it. His handshake is firm, but not overbearing. "Thanks for coming."

He puts his hands in his pockets and glances around the gallery. "Yeah, it's been fun to see the town again. It's been a long time. I read over the information you sent me, and I've been doing some research. Jetty Beach is a perfect place for some new development. I'll start with the gallery; this place has potential."

"You'll have to find out from the owners if they're interested in selling. But I have their contact information for you." I hand him a slip of paper.

He takes it and grins. "Sure. I'll make it worth their while."

What must it be like, to be able to buy anything you want?

"Anyway," he says. "This little town's a lot of fun. I'm glad I came down. I thought I'd get out of here today, but I think I'll stay the weekend. Maybe get a street taco."

He says that like he's never done it before. He probably hasn't. Don't rich people dine on filet mignon every night?

"Sounds great."

A woman in a sleek gray pantsuit walks into the gallery.

"Sorry to interrupt," she says. "Nicole Prescott?"

I'm pretty sure I recognize her voice. "Yes."

Jackson shakes my hand again. "Thanks, Nicole. It was nice to see you again."

"You too, Jackson." I turn to the woman as Jackson leaves. "Sorry."

"No, that's fine. I'm Mary Harper, the Tourism Director. We spoke on the phone several times, but I don't think we've met in person."

"Of course, Mary. It's nice to see you."

"You too. Listen, I wanted to tell you that you've done an amazing job with the festival. I'm really impressed."

"Thank you."

"I understand you did all this in your spare time, while still working in Seattle."

"That's true for the most part. Although I've been in town for the last couple of weeks, which made it easier to manage all the last minute details. It's been a little crazy, but also a lot of fun."

"That's great. We have a lot more events we'd like to produce for the town. So far, we haven't had the right person on staff to make it happen. Plus, there are plans for my organization to take over the art festival at some point. We didn't want to step on anyone's toes, so we've left it to the original organizers. But it sounds like, without you, the festival wouldn't have happened this year."

"Well, I've done my best."

"What are your plans after the festival is over? Do you have to go back to work in Seattle?"

"No, actually, I left my previous position. I'm still deciding what I'd like to do next."

Mary smiles and pulls out her business card. "That's great news. I'm looking for someone like you. I know you're busy, so I won't inundate you right now. But give me a call after the festival if you're interested. I might have a job for you."

I turn her card over in my hand, so surprised I'm not sure what to say. "Thank you. That's ... amazing."

"I hope to hear from you."

I shake her hand. "You will. Thank you."

Mary leaves and Melissa appears in the doorway. "Nicole, we need you out here. There's something going on."

The urgency in her voice almost makes me jump. "Okay, I'll be right there."

I hurry out the door, wondering what could possibly be wrong. The sky is clear, so it can't be rain. Did one of the banners hanging across Main Street fall and cause an accident? Did the electricity for the food trucks go out?

I stop in my tracks. One side of the closed-off street is lined with canopies, artists displaying their work. But on the other side I see a series of large canvases set on wooden easels. Vaguely, I'm aware of people congregating behind me, but I can't take my eyes off the display.

It's me.

The first is a photo of me on the beach, my hair blowing back in the wind. It's a close-up of my face, my eyes looking off into the distance.

I wander closer, passing the first canvas.

The second is a wider shot, taken from behind while I walk down the sand, my footsteps trailing behind me.

Next is me in Ryan's studio, sitting in the window, a cup of coffee held up to my chin. The lighting is soft, my eyes lowered, eyelashes brushing my cheeks.

I keep walking. Me in the window again, my eyes on the camera, a little smile on my face.

Me, smiling, my lips parted over my teeth.

Me, on the beach again, my head turned over my shoulder.

I walk on and the next is footsteps in the sand. Our footsteps. Ryan's and mine.

I glance around, looking for him. A knot of people follows me down the line of photos, keeping a bit of distance. But I don't see Ryan.

Cody and Hunter are on the edge of the crowd. Maureen is between them, and Ed behind her. Maureen clutches a little green handbag to her chest, a huge smile on her face. Next to them are my parents. Wait, what? Cody catches my eye and nods, gesturing for me to continue on.

My heart races and my tummy does little somersaults. There are four more canvases, all in a line, but they're covered with white cloths. I walk up to the first one, looking around again for Ryan. My hand trembles as I lift the cloth.

It's the beach, just in front of Ryan's house. Written on the sand is one word: *Will*

Oh my god.

I let the cloth flutter to the ground and move to the next canvas. The beach, another word written in the sand: *You*

The crowd lets out a collective gasp. I race over to the next canvas and whip off the cloth: *Marry*

Tears blur my vision. My hands are shaking so violently, I have a hard time clasping the edge of the cloth to reveal the final word: *Me*

I gasp and my hands fly up to my mouth. The crowd makes another noise and I feel the presence of someone right behind me.

I turn. Ryan stands there, that sweet, lopsided grin on his face. The cuffs of his white button-down shirt are rolled up. He adjusts his slacks as he slowly sinks down on one knee.

The *oohs* and *ahs* from the crowd fall away as Ryan takes my hand. He looks up at me, his green eyes glistening.

"Nicole Prescott, will you marry me?"

I laugh and cry all at once, unable to speak. He stands, slowly, and produces a small box, as if by magic. He opens it, revealing a beautiful diamond solitaire with a gold band. I hold out my hand—he has to hold it steady, I'm shaking so badly. I take a trembling breath as he slips the ring on my finger and looks into my eyes.

"Yes."

He stands and brings me in for a kiss and it's like my entire life clicks into place. This man. I love him so much, broken pieces and all. And now I'm going to spend the rest of my life loving him with everything I have.

AFTERWORD

Dear Reader,

I'm an overthinker by nature, and I thought about this book for a long time before I started writing it.

I knew I wanted to venture into a new genre, and romance was a natural fit. My favorite part of any story is usually the love story, whether it features heavily in the plot or not. I'm a sucker for a good will-they-or-won't-they, or will-it-work-or-won't-it story. But when it came to writing my own romance, I wasn't sure where to start.

I thought about whether I'd be able to write believable characters who were single and dating in their late twenties. I married my high school sweetheart, so my personal experience in the dating pool is pretty limited.

And that's when it hit me. What if my relationship hadn't worked? What if I'd dated my boyfriend for years, but we hadn't gotten married? And what if I found myself suddenly single, without much experience in the world of dating?

That's how I discovered Nicole. She's a woman who believed her life was headed in a certain direction—a very linear direction. When that reality comes crashing down, she's faced with navigating a world she didn't think she'd be a part of. She's insecure about the world of dating, and isn't sure how to handle a fledgling relationship.

I knew Ryan would be a photographer, and when I created his backstory, I knew he had suffered. Depression is a very serious illness, one that has touched people I love. I wanted to explore what happens when someone finds themselves relapsing, despite the presence of good things in their life. Part of Ryan's struggle is the feeling that he shouldn't be sad and listless because he has Nicole. The juxtaposition of the good with the dark makes his relapse deeper. He berates himself for not being happy, when the truth is, depression isn't about happiness. It's much more serious than a bad mood or feeling down. Ryan has to acknowledge this in order to take the steps necessary to pull himself out of the darkness again.

I raise a glass to anyone who has slogged through the mud of depression. The fact that you get up, day after day, working, playing, socializing, loving—even when it's so hard you're not sure you can—is a feat. You're brave as fuck and I salute you.

I hope you enjoyed this story. I loved writing it and already find myself missing these characters. The good news is, you'll get to see a little more of them in the next few Jetty Beach romances. I don't want to give too much away, but they did get engaged, so there will be a wedding down the road...

Thanks for reading!

CK

ALSO BY CLAIRE KINGSLEY

For a full and up-to-date listing of Claire Kingsley books visit
www.clairekingsleybooks.com/books/

For comprehensive reading order, visit
www.clairekingsleybooks.com/reading-order/

The Haven Brothers

Small-town romantic suspense with CK's signature endearing characters and heartwarming happily ever afters. Can be read as stand-alones.

Obsession Falls (Josiah and Audrey)

Storms and Secrets (Zachary and Marigold)

Temptation Trails (Garrett and Harper)

The rest of the Haven brothers will be getting their own happily ever afters!

How the Grump Saved Christmas (Elias and Isabelle)

A stand-alone, small-town Christmas romance.

The Bailey Brothers

Steamy, small-town family series with a dash of suspense. Five unruly brothers. Epic pranks. A quirky, feuding town. Big HEAs. Best read in order.

Protecting You (Asher and Grace part 1)

Fighting for Us (Asher and Grace part 2)

Unraveling Him (Evan and Fiona)

Rushing In (Gavin and Skylar)

Chasing Her Fire (Logan and Cara)

Rewriting the Stars (Levi and Annika)

The Miles Family

Sexy, sweet, funny, and heartfelt family series with a dash of suspense. Messy family. Epic bromance. Super romantic. Best read in order.

Broken Miles (Roland and Zoe)

Forbidden Miles (Brynn and Chase)

Reckless Miles (Cooper and Amelia)

Hidden Miles (Leo and Hannah)

Gaining Miles: A Miles Family Novella (Ben and Shannon)

Dirty Martini Running Club

Sexy, fun, feel-good romantic comedies with huge... hearts. Can be read as stand-alones.

Everly Dalton's Dating Disasters (Prequel with Everly, Hazel, and Nora)

Faking Ms. Right (Everly and Shepherd)

Falling for My Enemy (Hazel and Corban)

Marrying Mr. Wrong (Sophie and Cox)

Flirting with Forever (Nora and Dex)

Bluewater Billionaires

Hot romantic comedies. Lady billionaire BFFs and the badass heroes who love them. Can be read as stand-alones.

The Mogul and the Muscle (Cameron and Jude)

The Price of Scandal, Wild Open Hearts, and Crazy for Loving You

More Bluewater Billionaire shared-world romantic comedies by Lucy Score, Kathryn Nolan, and Pippa Grant

Bootleg Springs
by Claire Kingsley and Lucy Score

Hot and hilarious small-town romcom series with a dash of mystery and suspense. Best read in order.

Whiskey Chaser (Scarlett and Devlin)

Sidecar Crush (Jameson and Leah Mae)

Moonshine Kiss (Bowie and Cassidy)

Bourbon Bliss (June and George)

Gin Fling (Jonah and Shelby)

Highball Rush (Gibson and I can't tell you)

Book Boyfriends

Hot romcoms that will make you laugh and make you swoon. Can be read as stand-alones.

Book Boyfriend (Alex and Mia)

Cocky Roommate (Weston and Kendra)

Hot Single Dad (Caleb and Linnea)

Finding Ivy (William and Ivy)

A unique contemporary romance with a hint of mystery. Stand-alone.

His Heart (Sebastian and Brooke)

A poignant and emotionally intense story about grief, loss, and the transcendent power of love. Stand-alone.

The Always Series

Smoking hot, dirty talking bad boys with some angsty intensity. Can be read as stand-alones.

Always Have (Braxton and Kylie)

Always Will (Selene and Ronan)

Always Ever After (Braxton and Kylie)

The Jetty Beach Series

Sexy small-town romance series with swoony heroes, romantic HEAs, and lots of big feels. Can be read as stand-alones.

Behind His Eyes (Ryan and Nicole)
One Crazy Week (Melissa and Jackson)
Messy Perfect Love (Cody and Clover)
Operation Get Her Back (Hunter and Emma)
Weekend Fling (Finn and Juliet)
Good Girl Next Door (Lucas and Becca)
The Path to You (Gabriel and Sadie)

ABOUT THE AUTHOR

Claire Kingsley is a #1 Amazon bestselling author of sexy, heartwarming contemporary romance, romantic comedies, and small-town romantic suspense. She writes sassy, quirky heroines, swoony heroes who love big, romantic happily ever afters, and all the big feels.

She can't imagine life without coffee, great books, and the characters who inhabit her imagination. She lives in the inland Pacific Northwest with her three kids.

www.clairekingsleybooks.com

Made in the USA
Monee, IL
04 August 2025